An Old Wive's Tale

Amy Wonnacott

Copyright © 2023 Amy Wonnacott
All rights reserved.

For my darling Mummy. Sweet Caroline. I miss you.

"The good times never seemed so good." - Neil Diamond

1

Dear Jessica,

Mike says that they won't let you see me. I'm sorry about that. They have strict rules here. Attempting to garner a patient's story for public scrutiny is against their policy, especially when said patient is supposed to be mentally ill. It would open the floor to opinion. You know yourself that the press adopts a judgemental angle that invites the general public to act as judge, jury and executioner. I've seen it happen, innocent people dragged for crimes that they didn't commit, or minor celebrities flung into stories of abuse and cheating that eventually leads to a eulogy on the front page a few months later encouraging everyone to "be kind." We all lap up one side of a story without taking the time to communicate or understand both sides. In our hearts I think we love it; the drama or the intrigue.

I digress, this is not a slam piece on my opinion on the plights of the British press. This is supposed to be an earnest letter, one that's supposed to give you what you want. I may not have the energy that I used to have, and my arse may have appeared to have melted and reshaped the plastic of my seat, but I have had a lot of time to think about a variety of different things whilst I've been in here. All I am allowed to do is think. My thoughts are all mine, and I can think about what I like without consequence. I will admit I was about to throw your letter on top of the pile with the others. Within my 5 years at Fullingham, I have received hundreds of letters from journalists asking me various questions that were already intrusive from the first line. The Sun, online blogs, The Tab, even a man who claimed he was a "researcher" but was really hinting that he wanted me to do an "Ask me Anything" on some creepy subreddit. Every one of those went onto the pile and Mike, my orderly, came and took them away. Yours was different from the rest, as yours fell into my lap on the 5-year anniversary of my admission into Fullingham. Your language was strangely coy, like you couldn't quite make out just how unhinged I really was. When you really must think about how to phrase something, because you're worried that the person that you're talking to will take it the wrong way. I didn't take it the wrong way. In fact, I was intrigued by your offer. To publish my truth, in my own words. A lot of other journalists were promising a write up that I just couldn't trust, couldn't control. And if there is one thing that I cling to, one thing that was taken from me, it's control. The one opportunity you have given me to recount this myself is too magnanimous to pass up. I thought, as night draws in and life buzzes by, that if you couldn't come to me, then I would do my best to come to you.

For you to want to speak with me at all, you must already know a bit about my story. "Extraordinary", "Peculiar", words I read in online articles dedicated to deciding if I was really telling the truth or not. I wonder if you have decided already, pre-empted a decision that comes from your own research rather than my recollection. Other newspapers, their idea is entertainment, purely and simply. They barely report the truth anymore. Whatever is printed must sell. I can understand that. I don't pretend that I know much about the Exeter Herald, but I'm sure your readers will want to pick this one up for the pure fact that it is guaranteed drama-fuelled entertainment.

I take it you haven't ever visited a Psychiatric Hospital before. Maybe that's what put you off. I would be lying if I said that it didn't make me nervous at the prospect at first. Times have changed, and it isn't like an 80's horror flick anymore. The décor is just as you would expect. The walls are still a pasty shade of white and the floor still squeaks with every footstep, just as you would guess. Sometimes the bulbs flicker ominously in the overhead lights. Men in green scrubs laugh with receptionists in thick-rimmed glasses and rainbow lanyards. I sit in my room facing the window and despair that it won't open. I long for more air. Sometimes, when I'm bored, I'll pick at the seal with my nail until the crumbs cover the sill and I sweep them gently to the floor with my hand. Maybe one day I'll pick enough away that the window will swing open, like a prisoner chipping away at stone to create a getaway tunnel.

My day is boring in here. The lights flicker on at a measly 7am, burning my eyelids with their glaring ferocity. Mike bursts in, handing me a fresh pair of grey tracksuit bottoms and a white t-shirt. I was allowed to keep my favourite black hoodie (without the drawstrings, of course) and I wear it every day. I don't care that there is a crust of spilt toothpaste on the sleeve or a slither of soup on the chest. It's not like I have anywhere to be, anyone to impress.

Breakfast is in the dining hall, a ghastly room with disgusting ochre walls in an attempt to be "joyful". Posters peel from the paint and brown at the edges, encouraging art as therapy or advertising a lesser-known author coming to speak to the congregation in 2 weeks' time. The tables are slick wooden benches, pushed together to encourage communal eating. I sit on the end, eating dry muesli as slow as I can to make it last as long as I possibly can. I chew and chew until it turns to sticky mulch in my cheeks and tastes of nothing, then I swallow slowly and with intent. They must usher me out of the door, I won't give up the chance to sit in another seat looking at a different view of the outside. When I sit in this same spot, for breakfast, lunch and dinner, I get to watch the water on the fountain hit the marble and splash across the gravel. I watch as it turns to ice in the winter and provides a cooling mist in the Summer. I imagine what it would feel like to splash onto my skin.

11am is group therapy, followed by lunch at 12. By the time lunchtime rolls around, I am incredibly tired. From the cocktail of tablets, yes, but also from listening to everyone talk in succession as Dr Ralph encourages complete integrity. There is a mixed bag in here, from depressed teenagers to paranoid schizophrenics who are receiving the best possible treatment here. It is top in the country for a reason, and worth the price tag, as far as my mother is concerned. I don't say much in these meetings, mostly because even the most intense of fantasists sit and roll their eyes at my story. I save it for 1-to-1 therapy which happens after lunch, where Dr Ralph tries to encourage me to remember that sometimes the mind can alter memories every time you think them. Rewrite them, almost. We remember someone's t-shirt being a different colour, or that someone was wearing a hat when they weren't. It is normal for our brain to remember something differently every time we recount it.

Maybe then I will sit in the community room for a while. They normally have a Disney film on the television. Aladdin is my favourite. I have fond memories of watching that one with my Mum on a Sunday morning when I was little. In my pink fluffy pyjamas curled up on the sofa at her side, legs tucked under me like a cat. Fond memories of comfort and normalcy. If I'm lucky, they'll be an argument that I can listen to, or gossip from the orderlies about some of the other doctors. Who's going through a nasty divorce, which Doctor is carrying on with one of the nurses. It is relatively brainless, but as I'm only allowed on the internet in the computer room within certain time windows it's more entertaining than reading an old, battered version of Wuthering Heights over and over again until I am convinced that I am Cathy myself.

Time ticks on, as I wait for dinner to roll around. It comes at 5pm, and I'm the first in there, heaping mashed potato onto my plate like it's going to suddenly evaporate. Again, I roll eating out like it's a meal in a restaurant. Sipping my plastic cup of water like it's a gin and tonic, sloshing like It's just a little bit too strong for me to taste straight away. When it's over, I waddle back to my room with a slowness that feels dampened. Everything I do is long and drawn out. Slow and steady. Just picking up my feet to walk feels like the heaviest of tasks, like in the sole of my white plimsoll is a weight.

Even as I write this, every ten minutes two eyes peak through the flap in the door. I can see Mike's white irises peering through and resting on me for a split second, before disappearing for a while. Being here is like being in a big prison disguised as a country house. I take solace in the view from the window. A blue lake surrounded by vegetation. Sometimes, I get to see some ducks. Lights go out at 8pm, and then I'm plunged back into the darkness and stillness of being completely and entirely alone. I lay on my back and stare at the ceiling until my eyes start making out shapes in the dark that flash and swirl until I can't keep them open anymore. I fight sleep like it's toxic. I'm not writing to you to tell you about life at Fullingham, and I'm sure that you are wishing I would just get to the point. Although that might make a good expose for you, life in one of the UK's top psychiatric hospitals, it's not what you want to hear from me. I want you to imagine what life is like for me here. I was hoping to be out within a year, but Dr Ralph told my mother that I wasn't making enough progress in his sessions. Despite being on a concoction of different drugs, it wasn't enough to satisfy them that I was moving forward with my treatment. 5 years later, I'm still here, sat on this grainy plastic seat and staring at an outside that I wish I could understand. I won't leave my story behind and I won't lie for the sake of the Doctor's notes. I am nervous. I am nervous to say that it didn't happen in case I start to believe that I truly am losing my mind. It's all I have.

I want you to believe me, Jessica. If you are going to take my story and publish it then I want you to read everything with an open mind. I want you to stop wondering what's wrong with me and start wondering what is wrong with the world. All the bad things that happen that you can avoid, simply by burying your head in the sand and pretending that these things only happen in the movies. Or perhaps, far away on other continents. It is why I am here. The world is more fucked up than we can ever wrap our heads around. I see "inmates" in here with traumatic stories that have completely shattered their worldly perspective. I am one of those. I used to look at the world like it couldn't hurt me. I was shielded by a mother's unwavering love and the idea that I would eventually get what I always hoped for. How quickly we fall to the earth when we've been flying in the clouds for so long.

I am enclosing it all, the whole thing. If you have any questions, please do write back. I will receive it when Mike brings it in with the post.

I suppose I should start at the beginning, and it all started when Tom's Grandad died.

2

It was a wet June morning when the phone rang. The rain battered the windows fiercely, like a grey beast trying to break the glass, and had been keeping me awake since the early hours. I was already laying on my back, my eyes wide open, listening to what sounded like a drum being whacked over and over again. Methodically quiet, and then suddenly loud and fast. Although morning was approaching, through the small slit in the curtain folds I could see that the outside was still blanketed in darkness. Insomnia was not unfamiliar to me, although it tended to suck less on a Sunday morning rather than when I knew I had to get up for work.

The shrill of the phone did not even shake me, although a shock to hear at almost 6am on a Sunday.
Tom stirred next to me, groaning. It continued to ring out across the flat.
"Who the fuck is that?" Tom mumbled; his face buried into the pillow.
"Cold caller?" I suggested, monotonously.
"Shut up," Tom rolled over, yawning, "Go and get it?"
"Why me?"
"You're awake anyway, I know you are."
I sighed, about to make my stiff muscles do their job, when the telephone suddenly stopped.
"Well, there you are." I said, relieved.
The mechanical shrill started again. With a sigh I heaved myself out of my side of the bed and slowly stumbled out of the bedroom door and into the pitch black of the hallway. The carpet was crisp under my toes, bits and pieces of crumbs and the like sticking to the soles of my feet. I became increasingly aware that we needed to hoover.
The phone illuminated the hallway in the darkness, the little green screen showing nothing other than a number that I did not recognise. Someone was incredibly persistent

to be ringing the house phone that usually sat and gathered dust.

"Hello?" I croaked.

"Polly? Is Tom there?"

It was Tom's Sister, Lena. The tone of her voice was like a long sigh, drawn out and fed up. Which was immediately unusual.

"Uhhh, yeah, I'll wake him."

I put the phone down carelessly onto the side table, and craned my neck towards the bedroom door, "Tom!"

He groaned again, "What?"

"It's Lena."

"Tell her to ring back later."

"I think it's urgent, you should come and get it."

I heard the frustrated sound of the bed covers being thrown off, and Tom marching across the bedroom floor. He was always a moody git when he first woke up, rubbing sleep from his eyes like a toddler might. He picked up the phone and held it to his ear. His mouth was downturned, his eyes glossy and his hair like straw stuck with sweat against his forehead. He smelt like a barnyard.

"What is it, Lena? Its 6am!"

I watched as his expression loosened up. He was listening intently to the quiet high-pitched babble you could just

about make out down a phone line. Like a character in a video game.
"What?" He sounded defeated, I furrowed my brow. "When?"
I bit my lip, standing far enough back but close enough that I could try and make out some of what was being said.
"Grandad"
"Heart"
"Nightmare"
Whatever sentence these words were put into, was obviously going to be an incredibly disheartening one. Grandad. I thought about how inherently little I knew about Tom's Grandad except for the fact that he was once painter.
"Well, yes," Tom said, "We'll come as soon as we can. I just need to drop some bits off at Leo's on the way…no, it's fine."
In my mind, I had pieced enough together to get a vague gist of what was going on. The way Tom's face had lost its colour, the way Lena's voice had sounded more frantic and high-pitched as they continued to converse. Tom said his goodbyes, putting the phone down carefully. He didn't look up from the floor as he stepped back, putting his palm

against the wall and sighing deeply. His shoulders were hunched, like a great weight had been dropped upon them.
I hesitated, "Are you okay?"
"No," Tom answered quickly, "Grandad. He's gone."
"Gone?"
"He's dead, Polly."
I gasped, "How?"
"Heart attack." Tom rubbed his fingers on the bridge of his nose.

Tom and Lena were twins. Not identical. To start with, Lena was blonde, and Tom was brunette. Lena had a short and pointed nose like a pixie and Tom's nose was thick and angular. If you had put them in a room together and asked me, I wouldn't have guessed that they were related. Of course, I hadn't met Lena in person at this point, but I had seen a couple of photographs of the two of them together that helped me to decipher that they were two opposite sides of the spectrum. One academic, one creative. One energetic and outgoing and the other laid back and reserved. They even dressed differently, their aesthetics complete opposites. Tom was in favour of a pair of corduroys and a feathered flannel shirt, whereas Lena looked like she'd taken her inspiration from the pages of Marie Claire.

Tom was pushing 30, and his Grandad had still endeavoured to call him every week to check he was alright. The phone calls were short and hushed, and always with his love passed on to me. We had never met, but I was warmed by the idea that he still thought about me and wished me well. That was the sign of someone with a sweet disposition.

I sniffed, "We ought to go, Tom. We better get there."

"Yeah," Tom sniffed too, I hadn't ever seen him cry, but he looked like he was about too, "Just pack some things."

Tom and Lena's Grandad had raised them after their parents died in a car accident when they were small. Conan, Tom's Grandad, had been through a messy divorce himself and had no contact with his ex-wife, so brought the two of them up on his own as a single parent. That was as much as I knew of Tom's upbringing as he wouldn't let me in on emotional matters. He rarely spoke of his parents, only enough to tell me that he barely remembered them at all.

He was like that ever since we first met each other. It was 5 years prior, and we were at a wedding. I was fresh and hopeful at 21 and I was working at a law firm. My intentions were to work my way up the ladder and make it to a prominent position without having to go through university. This was much to my mother's dismay. My Mother, Mimi Newton, was a university lecturer. She taught English Literature to a hoard of budding academics that favoured and almost fantasised over her works. Some of her books you may have heard of as a writer yourself, such as *"Way of Wings"* and *"Children of the Caves."* I must confess, I haven't read *Children of the Caves*, but I often pretend I have done. Mum would beg me to come to the graduations and watch as her students paraded across the stage clutching a scroll and smiling sweetly and pretending they hadn't just drunk away thousands of pounds that they wouldn't be able to pay back. I think it was a desperate attempt to try and convince me to get a degree. I didn't see the point in it, when I could work and make money from the beginning without a debt. I wanted to be a lawyer, and the longer it went on the more I wanted to prove to my Mum that I could do it on my own. It was definitely more difficult to get to the role that I wanted without a law degree, but it wasn't impossible. Like I said, I was hopeful.

I didn't admit it at the time, but I also didn't want to go to university because I struggled socially. I was told at school by a group of prepubescent boys that I was "weird", and I hadn't been able to get that out of my head since. It hung over me with every social interaction, every new friend or work colleague. My immediate assumption was that they would think I was weird and discuss my weird antics behind my back. In the essence of avoiding paranoia, I would keep people at arm's length unless they forced me close. I would cling onto those who dared to get close enough and fret that they would eventually leave too. Dr Ralph takes great grandeur pleasure in unpacking this at every session. He tells me that I have social anxiety with an anxious attachment style which, at this point, just adds to everything else. Going to University is all about first impressions, and if you don't make friends in the first week you are forced to the back-burner to rot in a library and pretend that you have some importance in what you are undertaking. It was only when I started at the firm that I learnt the importance of faking it and could stand up in a courtroom and state the facts with poise. I didn't have to pretend.

It didn't help that my father was also a university lecturer. I never met him. He disappeared on sabbatical when my mother was pregnant with me, and the only story she has ever told me was a fairy story about him living on the Galapagos Islands and studying birds. It's hard to miss something that you never had. Some people will look at others and long for what they have, but I was content with the way things were with Mum and I. I grew up in a townhouse in Reigate with a green front door, and I used to bask in the fact that it was just the two of us in a big house. Mum loved maximalism. Everything had its place in amongst the paint splatters on canvas and Habitat rugs. I used to sit on the boucle cuddle seat in the window with my headphones on, watching the cars go by and staring at the oval topiary as its loose leaves fluttered in the wind in our front garden. I loved the cosiness of our digs. I loved the fire that roared in the winter and the wind-chimes that tinkled in the summer by the open window. Mum took pride in her home style, the only place that resembled disorganisation was the study. Mum kept a picture of my father on the desk, in amongst the scattered piles of paperwork and fraying books. He looked nothing like me.

At this stage of my life, where I met Tom for the first time, I remember feeling young and more carefree. I'd work hard in the week and go out with my work colleagues at the weekend. Most of my small handful of school friends had gone off to university or travelling or had moved into London. I relied heavily on the social life of my work friends, most of whom were older than I was and more mature. I felt my "social anxiety" start to waiver when I realised that they were old enough that they didn't care that whether I watched anime on Netflix in my spare time or preferred to wear minimal makeup over a full face. Schoolgirl plights were nothing in the adult world. I learnt how to indulge in conversation and disappear when my social battery ran out. I thought I was an introvert. One of my friends from work, Jade, asked me to be her bridesmaid. I met her on my first day and she had immediately taken a liking to me, forcing me to go to house parties with her or go to the pub for one glass of red wine that ended in 2 bottles. The fact that we were of opposite personalities only drew me to her more. She was older than me and had been engaged for a long while. The wedding was at a converted barn just outside of Reigate and my Mum was invited too. She loved Jade and so did I, she had a way of charming everyone that she met.

Tom was the photographer. It always made sense to me that this was his chosen profession. He was the quiet type, behind the camera and not in front of it. Lurking away capturing moments of strength and weakness and joy and jealousy. Photographers blend in, and all the guests see is the flash of the bulb. He had a lightness to his step. You didn't even notice he was there.

I did though. That first time I noticed him he was behind his lens, snapping a photo of Jade and I as well as the other bridesmaids. He had been there all morning, but I was too enveloped in my duties to notice him flittering about. Champagne flowed and I do, looking back, believe that the champagne hindered my ability to think straight as I looked into his eyes the first time. My heart pumped in my throat like it was going to jump straight out of my mouth. I could see the spark as our gaze connected, electricity buzzed in the air as all I wanted to do was touch him. It was a feeling that I was unfamiliar with. I had never been in a relationship with anyone and the only intimacy I was familiar with was awkward hookups at parties I had gone to with Jade. I could barely look a lover in the eye. With Tom, I couldn't look *away* from his eyes.

He was so good looking. A cheeky smile that was charming and alluring and sucked me straight in. He was wearing a crisp white shirt, held together at the neck by a red bowtie. His trousers were tan, neat slacks. I took him in as he refocused his camera on me and pressed the button, *click*. Still at the bottom of the pecking order in every other aspect of my life, I wanted to be at the top of this one. That strangely quiet demeanour he was oozing didn't last very long, because at the end of the night he was fucking me behind a tree at the bottom of the farm orchard. His lips tasted like a combination of tobacco and sweet craft beer.

The talking stage was tumultuous and at times he would often take days to reply. At one point, Jade told me to block him immediately and not waste my time. I was so drawn in by him that the thought of completely dismissing him made my chest ache. I didn't recognise myself, checking my phone every few minutes and getting frustrated when the same unchanged wallpaper glared back at me. No new notifications. When we would meet, he was holding something back. When we fucked, we were closer than ever, and I felt the love flow through me and engulf me as I looked up at him. I would try to tell him how much I loved him and wanted him through the desperation in my eyes, or through our lustful kisses. I held him so close that my fingernails made crescent moons in his shoulders. He would withhold touch when we were in public, only holding my hand under the table or stroking my calf with his palm. I wanted him to stay by my side. I tried to ignore the fact that at first, he would only text me after 10pm. I told myself that no one had ever cared for me like that before. His words would drip with promises and a future that I saw for myself, a marriage and family like Jade was creating. It was my time now. He didn't seem to care that I was quieter than he was, or that I was in my own head sometimes. He also didn't seem to care that I spent a lot of time reading with my headphones in instead of playing a sport or doing something active. I liked being stationary as much as I liked watching law documentaries. As time went on in our weird relationship, seeing each other turned into a daytime activity as well as just a nighttime activity. Tom would play football on a Saturday morning, and I would lay in bed until mid-morning before slouching about in my pyjamas on the sofa waiting for him to pick me up and take me out for lunch. He'd always have a cup of tea with my Mum whilst he waited for me to get dressed.

Five years after Jade's wedding, here I was standing in our flat in Guildford at 6 in the morning, trying to console him the best I could when that wasn't something that came so naturally to me.
I could still hear the rain on the windows, hammering away like needles on the glass. Tom was in his study packing his gear ready to drop at Leo's on the way. My suitcase sat upright and ominous in the corner, my duffle bag deflating against my leg.

I called my Mum.

"Polly?" My Mum answered on the second ring, "It's a bit early for you, isn't it?"
"Tom's Grandfather died, Mum," I whispered, "I have to go to Cornwall for a while."
"I'm so sorry to hear that, darling," She sighed, "How is he?"
"Weirdly, he seems relatively calm."
"That will change. Grief feels easy to defeat until it rears its ugly head."
My Mum was dramatic, poetic. I wondered which book she had lifted that from.
"I have to go. I will call you tomorrow?"

"Have you spoken to Chase?" Chase was my boss.
"I'll call him tonight. I have holiday left, I'm sure he won't mind me using it."
Mum passed on her condolences and then left me alone again. Tom was ready, carrying 2 camera bags and a laptop bag full of cables. He didn't say much as we took the stairs and ran out to the car, we still got soaked in only a short distance.

"Typical, isn't it? Rain in June?" I tried.

Tom didn't respond.

The silence continued on the way to Leo's, across town. Leo came to the door in raggedy pyjama trousers and a holey nirvana t-shirt. He looked pissed that he'd been woken this early.

Leo was Tom's apprentice. Well, he had grown into more of a business partner. They teamed up at weddings as a first and second shooter. Leo was a nice guy, albeit slightly naïve. He didn't care much for the photographs but enjoyed the praise that came from being naturally gifted at something.

With Leo's house fading into the blur of the rain on the rear window, we took to the motorway and watched as Surrey was left behind. The sky lightened with every mile we travelled. Early morning sun began to break through the grey clouds and turn the damp ground into a thick dust. I did vaguely know where I was going. Tom had spoken about where he had grown up in a very ambiguous way. Like he wanted to forget but simultaneously remember, keeping his hometown on the cusp of his memory so that he could reach for it if he needed but push it away if it swayed too close. We hadn't ever visited as a couple.

Mountmend, as Tom had explained it, was a Cornish village just outside of Bodmin surrounded by woodland. It sat deep in the middle of nowhere, with the closest supermarket being about half an hour drive away. I grew up in Reigate. I had no experience of village life or what it was like out in the sticks like that. I tried to imagine what the draw was for Conan or Lena or Tom. I hadn't seen the beauty of some of the landscapes, and it *was* beautiful. But I had been to St Ives to visit the Tate, not to the small towns and villages in the heart of the county where only a handful of people resided. St Ives was bustling and touristic. The rest of Cornwall was a bit of an enigma for me. My mind conjured up images of Cornish pasties and cream teas, coves and boats and sea shanties. A massive stereotype that most Cornish people would probably object to. But that wasn't wrong, as I did eat my fair share of delicious pasties when I visited and there was a boat race off the harbour over the weekend that Mum and I stayed there. Fisherman with wide-brimmed anorak hats cast their vessels out beside men in tight gilets as people waved and cheered from the promenade. It was certainly charming.

We reached Mountmend by mid-morning. For at least an hour before we came to a halt, it was winding roads, tall trees and endless rolling fields. Pulling over into ditches for other cars to pass by and rolling out of them with a harsh bump. When we were close, a wooden sign that could have used another lick of paint pointed in the direction of Mountmend. We didn't take the town road, but instead a dusty side road that twisted into an expansive gravel yard. A stance of a foreboding white ranch house sat ahead of us. The stone was washed and faded, thick with build up from years of standing in that exact spot. It was over two floors, and the rectangular windows were large enough that you could catch a glimmer of what was inside, like it was teasing you and beckoning you in. The porch was covered in thick vines that snaked through to the roof, covering every crack and crevice that time had etched into its structure. I could see leaves built up in the gutters, damp seeping through the wooden steps. As I stepped out of the car, behind me dropped into a vast forest that appeared to stretch for miles and miles. Fluffy tips of trees created a carpet that disappeared off into the distance and onto hillsides and asperous terrain. It was worlds away from our built-up apartment building in suburban Guildford surrounded by carparks and roundabouts.

There was another car, a ford focus, parked in front of a wooden shed in disrepair. I looked at Tom for his explanation, but he was still in a silent reverie. He had barely looked in my direction for the 3-hour car journey and I had just found myself scrolling aimlessly on my phone and dealing with the headache from my travel sickness. It was not unusual for him not to speak to me for extended periods, but this car journey was particularly painful. Any attempts at making conversation were shot down quicker than they had left my mouth. Tom was like this naturally. He withdrew into himself when something was on his mind, and I found myself drained in attempts to try and drag his issues out of him. He was usually the talkative one who excelled in social situations, so it was obvious to me when something was truly bothering him when he became sullen and withdrawn. The air was thicker than a concrete block when both of us were going through quieter spells. I knew the issue this time, so I let it go. People grieve in different ways, Tom obviously grieved by ignoring those closest to him.

Tom pulled my case from the backseat, and I swung my duffel over my shoulder. He was making his way to the front door faster than I who struggled over the gravel.

The door swung open before Tom had even made it up the steps, and a woman rushed out throwing her arms around him with such a force that almost knocked him backwards. I jumped forward ready to catch my case if it took a dive.
"Tom, thank goodness. Are you alright?"
Tom held her back at arm's length, "As alright as I can be."
I recognised her quickly as Lena. She looked the same as she had done in her photographs, except she was taller than I imagined, matching Tom's height. Her hair was

slung back into a sleek ponytail that made her face look more defined, pulling her skin tighter. There was not a blemish, nor a wrinkle. A grey polo-neck hugged her chin, tucked into a long black skirt that looked like crimped satin. Lena looked like she'd stepped out of Woman's Weekly and directly onto the porch. I was intimidated by her as I pulled at the bottom of my grey sweatshirt. I glanced down quickly at the hole in my leggings. She noticed me over Tom's shoulder and stepped back, surprised.

"I did wonder when I would get to finally meet you," Lena took the steps and bounded towards me, her long skirt sticking to her legs, "You are even more stunning than I thought you would be."

I smiled, "And so are you. It's lovely to meet you in person."

She pulled me in for a hug. She smelt like a blend of burnt timber and lavender. So incredibly niche, but it surprisingly worked and added to her enticing nature. Her embrace felt instantly comforting.

"It's a shame it isn't under better circumstances." Lena smiled sadly. Her eyes were red and puffy. She was right, it was a shame that it had taken something so sinister for Tom to finally let me into this part of his life. *5 years*.

"What happened?" Tom started to move into the house and Lena hopped lightly up the stairs after him.
"It was late last night, I'm not sure when. Mr Oates called round to drop off some more feed for the chickens and he found him in the chair out back." Lena croaked.

Conan Baker's house was a mismatch of eras and full of knickknacks that made no sense where they were placed. In the hallway, a Persian rug with fraying edges sat dusty atop the floor. The walls were papered with an orange hexagonal print, adorned with black and white photos that had faded in the sunlight from the one long window and were now almost ochre. It was chaotic, an interior designer's worst nightmare. I don't pretend to know much about decorating, but even I had to take a deep breath when I was taking it all in. The house was rickety and full of splinters, with jagged shards of wood sticking up at the corners like an animal had scratched at it. I dropped my bag at the foot of the stairs and followed Tom and Lena through the living room and into a classic country kitchen that still had an aga. Ornamental dogs, a large wicker chicken, and a lamp with a shade made from cow-skin. There was a lot to unpack, interior wise.

"We're going to have to call Mr Ward." Tom suggested, hitting the button on the kettle.
"I've called him already."
"Who is Mr Ward?" I asked, reminding them both of my presence.
Tom ignored me, Lena smiled sympathetically, "He's the pastor."
I nodded.
"Where do we even start with this stuff?" Tom pulled open a kitchen drawer, "We need to get the house ready and it's in no fit state, is it?"
"Well, Arthur is coming up here in an hour or so to help sort things out."
Tom tutted, "How is he?"
"Don't," Lena sighed, flicking her wrist at nothing in the air, "Just, don't."

I stood there, in the doorway like a statue that had just become one of Conan's random ornaments. I wracked my brain to remember that Arthur was Lena's husband, but I couldn't recall ever seeing a picture of him before, so I drew a blank swiftly. I would learn that Arthur Penhallow was a plumber, 15 years Lena's senior.

I felt odd, stood in the kitchen of a dead man that I had not known, surrounded by all his things. I didn't know Conan enough to be invading his privacy like this. Tom and Lena continued to converse like it was the most natural thing in the world and I was on the outskirts looking in, wondering what happens now. I felt like an imposter. Have you ever attended a wedding as a plus one where you exclusively don't know anyone except the person who invited you? That's what it felt like. Awkwardly lingering and making it seem like you were looking at nothing and everything. Pretending that you're comfortable in being solitary whilst your partner catches up with people that you don't know. Resisting the urge to clear your throat. Tom suggested that Lena could take me, and I realised that I didn't know what he was talking about and that I had completely shut myself off from the conversation.

"Where am I going?" I said.

"I'll take you into the village, I've been here since late last night so I'm just going to change clothes. We'll pick up some food, you will know what you like, won't you?" Lena smiled, picking up her handbag from the large, oak dented dining table sat in the middle of the kitchen. She made it sound like I didn't really have a choice.

"Sure." I said.
Tom looked at me for the first time since we had left, his eyes glazed over, "I'll see you later?"
I nodded, grinning shyly.

The car ride wasn't the slightest bit awkward because Lena was an expert at making conversation where there was none. I was clearly overwhelmed, like a baby rabbit amongst foxes, she could smell the uncomfortable energy exuding from my sweat. She asked me about my job, and my family and friends. She asked me whether Tom had proposed yet, and I said that Tom had proposed to me on the beach in Tulum, Mexico, but I hadn't picked a ring yet. She was astonished that he was letting me choose and not doing it the "old fashioned way". I hadn't really thought about it like that, because it didn't scream to me that Tom didn't know me well enough to choose a ring. It told me that he knew me well enough to know that I would want to pick myself. I didn't buy into a lot of "traditions". So many are outdated and tedious, some even sexist. Lena looked like a traditionalist, so I didn't enter that discussion with her. We cycled through other topics quicker than I could respond. I was confused as to why she was preaching traditional values at me when her marriage to Arthur sounded like it was a complete set up. He was a friend of Conan's. It was exhausting, but I did welcome the conversation after the awkward silences of the car journey the night before.

As we drove through Mountmend that day, I realised that what I had imagined that the village would look like wasn't far from the truth. There was a small high street surrounding a triangular shaped green with a duck pond seemingly out of place in the middle. It looked like it had just been put there to add the essence of some greenery and to encourage some native wildlife. I counted a post office and a corner shop. I could see a bakery with a chalkboard standing on the pavement advertising "fresh bread". A tall, sleek, stone church spire could be seen poking out from behind the trees of a side lane aptly named "Church Lane". The Village was sleepy. I couldn't see a bar, but I could see a pub called "The Swan", Elizabethan in style with old, tattered benches scattered outside.

People seemed to mill about with not much of a care or sense of urgency. Lena was pointing people out like it was a game. "That's Mr Oates," She'd exclaim, "He was my teacher in Year 5. He also coached the cricket team that

Tom used to play for." The man that she was pointing to looked the same as every other man walking the street, with a cane and some type of hat. There was Mr Polkinghorne, the Farmer who they nicknamed "Horney" and Mrs Kestle, who Lena told me had 10 dogs. The professionalism with which they were referred to was unmatched, and no first names were mentioned besides "Perky Peter", who was a drunk who spent all day on the green by the pond drowning in a sea of liquor. It was a different world, where everyone knew each other and all their business. I couldn't even have told you what gender the upstairs neighbours were at home, let alone their professions or how many dogs they had.

We pulled up to a small street with a red brick detached town house perched right on the corner. It looked new compared to the other houses we had seen, especially Conan's. It had black metal fencing around the perimeter which was brought together by a gate, and you could see the floral drapes hanging proudly in the windows. The appearance of the house itself was just as pristine as Lena. The front garden had no individuality, the grass cut to within an inch of its life so that every blade was the same height. It looked like something out of a magazine. Not Country Living, more Modern Home. Lena pulled round the back into a driveway with a garage at the end and hopped out of the car. She strode in through the back gate and up a waxed garden path without waiting a moment for me to catch up. Her strides were long and strong. The garden smelt freshly mowed and echoed the sentiment of its front garden counterpart. There was nothing to make it stand out. I thought of the garden back at my Mum's house. The cohort of gnomes that sat in a regimental line in front of the conservatory window, a chipped birdbath, hoards of geraniums and petunias lining the outside fence. Mum used to spend every Sunday morning in her embroidered sunhat on her garden kneeler digging away.

Inside the house was like a show-home. Like they were expecting visitors at any moment. Everything was an elegant shade of grey with shiny silver handles, dark granite worktops glistened under the sun's rays. Her kitchen would be at the envy of any designer. It was certainly rungs above mine. All surfaces were slick and clean, not a crumb in site. The only appliance on the counter was a solitary grey kettle that looked expensive.

Lena dropped her bag on the kitchen island and strode over the fridge, "Would you like something to drink?"

I was suddenly very aware that my throat was dry and that I hadn't had a drink since the night before. "Please," I cleared my throat, "Some water."
She turned on the tap.
"Polly," She whispered, "I know this is a bit…scary, but I'm sure Tom appreciates having you here to support him right now."
I took the glass from her outstretched hand and sipped slowly. It was refreshingly cold. It was also clear, I noticed she hadn't needed to run the tap for 30 seconds to get rid of the chalky, cloudy colour.
"I'm not sure he's that bothered right now." I joked. My face must have not echoed the words that left my mouth. It did a stark job at giving me away at times.
"That's just Tom," She waved my thoughts away with her hand, "He doesn't know how to process emotion. You just must let him deal with it in his own way."
I nodded. He certainly was hard to read, but his quiet spells were something that I was very much used to.
"I'm going to have a quick shower and change," Lena headed towards the door, "Make yourself at home. The TV is through there and the remote is on the coffee table."

Lena was not long. 20 minutes at most. I wanted to snoop a little bit as her belongings stood out to me as more expensive than mine could ever hope to be. Her living room was painted a silvery ash, complete with a cream linen sofa scattered with lilac throw pillows. She had a white marble fireplace with photos of her and Tom atop. They were sweet children, playing in a sandbox in someone's back garden. It was strange seeing photos of Tom as a child as I had seen so little. I felt estranged from that part of his life, like he'd been born when I'd met him. He looked happy, beaming away with a spade in one hand a fist full of sand in the other. They were model children, like butter wouldn't melt. On the other side of the mantel was a picture of Lena and an older gentleman, his eyebrows bushier and his hair greying and smoothed back with so much gel it almost glistened. Arthur, Lena's husband.

I mentioned that Arthur was a plumber and miles older than Lena, and I later learned that Lena hadn't been all that keen in their companionship. Lena could have modelled for Glamour, whereas Arthur looked like the type of man you would see hunched over the bar at 11am in the local Wetherspoons. Next to each other, they looked like Father and Daughter. Strangely, Arthur had been one of Lena's late Father's good friends. I was intrigued to comprehend what she saw in him, but I never did. Dr Ralph would probably say that it was the absence of her Father that made Arthur such a viable option for her. I assume now that it was more a marriage of security and convenience, which gave Lena the nice house, the nice car and expensive accessories that others could envy. It was easy. I had watched all my life as people took the route that was most secure, rather than taking a risk. I was one of those people.

The weirdest part of Lena's décor caught my eye, and I felt my eyebrow furrow. In the middle of the mantelpiece taking centre stage was a strange circle of vines and twigs, looped together to make a bizarre organic ornament. It looked like a forest halo. I stretched out my hand to touch it and my fingertips brushed lightly against the rough twigs. It was a shock that it was real. The leaves felt smooth and firm, like they'd been kept fresh. It resembled something that you might make in an art lesson for adults at the local college, and I smiled gently at the thought that Lena probably wouldn't have been caught at an art class. This was definitely shop bought. I mention this for a reason, and I wish, Jessica, that you will remember that everything else in Lena's living room was pristine. It was all made of marble, sleek and shiny. Why would a ring of twigs be sitting so prominently in her space? Stick with me.

We did drive out of town to a little supermarket and brought some food to last Tom and I for at least a week. I quickly forgot about the twigs and Lena's house as my mind was quickly reminded of my rumbling stomach. I picked mostly comfort foods, donuts, crisps, frozen pizzas. I knew Tom would appreciate what he called "quick" food when he really wasn't in the right mindset to eat.

When we got back to the house, Arthur was there. His land rover was parked outside, next to where we parked Lena's Ford.

Tom had pulled cardboard boxes from the shed outside and erected them in the kitchen. Nothing sat inside them yet. They sat scattered across the kitchen table.

"Hello," Arthur looked chuffed when she saw me, "Who have we here then?"

Before I could answer, Lena jumped in, "This is Polly, Tom's Fiancée." It was still weird to hear myself referred to as a "fiancée" when I didn't even have a ring on my finger.

"Oh, how excellent!" Arthur pulled me forward for a hug. I was stiff as a board enveloped in his arms. I was baffled by his demeanour. He reminded me of my own grandfather, again the question came to mind as to what she was doing married to him. She was lean, blonde and youthful. She was the ultimate by today's beauty standards, a beautiful woman with confidence, brains and the ability to care for people. Arthur patted me lightly on the shoulder and moved through to the living room. Tom was sorting through a cupboard, pulling out tinned goods and lining them up on the counter.

"Hey." I tried, moving towards him.

He looked at me and relaxed a bit, smiling, "Hey."

"You okay?"

"Not really, but I must carry on with this. Did you get what you needed?"

"Yes, I think you'll be pleased with what we bought."

"I don't doubt it." He touched my cheek gently before getting back to his task.

I picked up a tin of rice pudding and was shocked to see the date printed on the side, 5th October 2000.
"Is this…?" I couldn't finish, I just held the can up to Tom with a look of disgust on my face.
Tom sighed, "I know. All of them are like it. He was a bit of a hoarder."
I put the can down and wiped a hand on my jeans. I glanced around me. This chaos of clutter should have made decade old tins predictable.

I didn't want to get in the way. Just as I was about to go and unpack in the guest bedroom and take a quick shower, the doorbell rang.
Arthur answered it, and there was the sound of a curt male voice echoing through the house. Tom stopped what he was doing, and I followed him through to the hallway to stand besides Lena.
"Tom!" exclaimed the man standing in the doorway, "It is always a pleasure to see you. It's a shame that it isn't a visit under a more positive circumstance."
"Thank you, Mr Ward. It is nice to see some friendly faces at the moment."

It was Mr Ward. The pastor.

A smaller woman stood by his side wearing a white dress with red roses scattered across the print, a thin shawl wrapped loosely around her shoulders. Her husband stood next to her looking like a giant in her wake. He was lanky, his shoulders appeared to hunch of their own accord like he'd spent years ducking under doorways. He was wearing nude linen trousers and a white shirt. They looked like they were both about to embark on an over 60s cruise around the Mediterranean.

"And who might this be?" Mr Ward gestured to me. In his hands he held what looked like a crumble. I drew a breath, it smelt like apple.

Lena spoke up this time, "This is Polly, Tom's fiancée."

Mr Ward looked shocked, "Fiancée? what a lovely surprise to see that you have found someone so special, Tom." His face was gaunt, dark patches under his cheekbones revealed more of the shape of his skull than you were supposed to see. He also had thin lips that he kept licking. The slapping noise was jarring. I noticed his yellow hair was receding further than he would have probably liked. No amount of gel could have fixed the fact that it was patchy.

Tom smiled, "Yes, it is her first time in Mountmend." I said nothing, offering nothing except a small smile. Mr Ward's beady eyes made me feel uncomfortable. I shifted from foot to foot.
He chuckled, "It is a lovely village, I hope you enjoy it for all it has to offer."
Arthur offered to take the crumble from Mr Ward's hands, and he seemed to remember where he was, "Ahhh yes. This is for you. Helen and I thought we would come up to pass on our condolences and check on you. Conan was a dear friend, and I was horrified to hear of his passing."
"Thank you, Clement," Arthur spoke this time, his voice thick with sadness, "We are all devastated."
"We were wondering if you would be kind enough to lead the service. If it is not too painful." Tom said.
I looked at him. His voice was formal like he was talking to a headteacher or a drill sergeant, he had his hands clasped in front of him like he was nervous. I kept waiting for him to address Mr Ward as "sir." I had not heard him speak to anyone this way.
"Absolutely, it would be an honour." Clement smiled tightly, like it was too much for his face muscles to be smiling for so long.

There was an awkwardness before Clement Ward took his leave, waving goodbye and offering his help should anything arise with the twins. They were both thankful. Each of them stood straight like soldiers and I was half expecting a salute. The energy in the air was thick with formality. I even felt myself straighten my spine, lift my chin. I had only felt this level of pressure when I was standing in front of a judge in the courtroom.

Off he went with his wife down the road, kicking up the gravel with his loafers as he walked. Their arms linked together. They were interesting, a demographic that I rarely encountered at home. I wasn't unfamiliar with money. My Mum had worked hard for plenty. Where there were floaty chiffon skirts, chinos and trips to the South of France with these two, my Mum was more of a vintage blazer and whiskey in Edinburgh type. Helen and Clement seemed to float, like they were being carried on the air of their status and bank balance. It is infuriating. At least I find that in Fullingham, everyone wears the same uniform and the only difference more money provides you with is an extra chocolate bar on a Friday. In some strange, anti-capitalist way I enjoy the equal playing field. I feel less like an avocado eating millennial and more like I'm living in a new-age movie.

Through the living room window, I watched Clement and Helen Ward walk away. Nobody else noticed, but he looked back at me standing curiously in the light of the window. I could have sworn I saw him wink.

3

Have you ever had to organise a funeral, Jessica? It's something that you don't envision yourself doing. It's not something that you imagine from the age of 5, like a wedding or a big birthday. Generally, you have no idea how it works until you must sort one and all of a sudden you realise that it's a business like everything else. There was something mildly grotesque and uncomfortable about having to choose the wood type for a coffin or choosing a suit and bowtie that someone will be wearing for what is essentially all eternity. Conan's funeral desires were simple. A ceremony at the church and a burial in the cemetery next to his Father. Generations of Conan's family all descending from Mountmend and buried in the same graveyard.

Tom went into the village to meet with Mr Ward that next day. The plot was to be made ready and the sermon finalised, and I didn't want to get involved more than I already had. I already felt like I was trespassing within a family affair that had nothing to do with me.

Tom dropped me off outside of the post office, handing me a fiver to pick up some lunch and a coffee. I queried the use of hard cash, but Tom said that card payments were rarely used in the village. I found that absolutely Edwardian, but I let it go. I felt like a shell of myself as I hopped from the car, Tom speeding off before I had a moment to think. My eyes felt crusty with insomnia, my failure to get comfortable in someone else's bed. In someone else's town. I wasn't unfamiliar with the overwhelming heavy feeling of being tired, but it felt so much worse when you were so far from home. I pulled at my flannel shirt and wrapped my arms tightly around my waist. I felt like I was suddenly under a magnifying glass, eyes falling on me as I stepped. I was a myth, a farce. It was evident that the townsfolk of Mountmend were not used to seeing visitors. I knew that I stood out like a sore thumb. I could feel the familiar hum of anxiety as it began to buzz in my toes and travelled up my legs into my stomach. It churned. I needed to eat something.

The village itself was even greyer up close. Grey bricks and stone, grey mortar. When you walk down the street in Guildford, there is a discernible character that comes with the black and white old school feel and the red brick buildings with bay windows. Mountmend had one building with flair, and that was its pub. The rest of its architecture was tired, like it had let out one final sigh before settling into a permanent state of weariness. I didn't find it endearing like a sleepy village in Sussex or by the sea, it had a different aura. The places I had visited in Cornwall were lined with pleasant cobblestone streets and cute houses meandering up hillsides. Mountmend was plain and flat.

I forgot how to walk normally as I made my way down the road. I was thinking too much. I tried to ignore the old lady who had stopped, walking stick hovering, to stare at me as I stopped on the other side of the village green outside a bakery. I hovered by the door. Two men in tweed flat-caps paused mid conversation to glare in my direction.

There was an eerie silence. Time ticked by so slowly that I could have sworn I could hear every second as it passed. They didn't look away as our eyes locked and a shiver rolled down my spine. I tried to focus on finding the handle for the door. I was already on edge, and I could feel my neck stiffen and tension in my shoulders. I immediately wanted to run back to Conan's house and not return to the village again. I took a deep breath, in through my mouth and out through my nose. My sense of smell was flooded with the aroma of freshly baked goods. It did smell delightful, and the vast array of wares in the window surprised me. I finally stepped inside and a small round, red-faced man behind the counter didn't smile as I awkwardly waved hello.
"Yes?" He bit.
I was taken aback. His tone was sharp.
I cleared my throat, "Uh, please can I get 2 sausage rolls and a white coffee?"
He sniffed, "And?"
"That's it."
He started bagging it up and the jingling bell on the door went off behind me.
"Hello Patrick." A woman's voice.

"Hello my dear, what can I get for you today? How's Todd?"

His tone had completely changed. I was standing there with a fiver in my hand, my sausage rolls sitting on the countertop waiting for the business exchange to happen. He made a beeline for the lady who had entered, her trench coat done up to the chin and a woolly hat on in Spring. You could see the sweat pooling on her forehead. I waited patiently as they conversed, but I felt awkward too. Without Tom I felt completely invisible. Outside, I was like a beacon that nobody could look away from. Inside the shop, I was nobody. When it came to actually conversing with me the air was thick with animosity. Patrick, the baker, took the note from my hand without looking at me. I dithered for my change, but then gave up and just swiped the sausage rolls from the counter and ducked out.

I waited for Tom on the bench opposite the pond. I internally begged for him to hurry up, focusing on the ducks that swam and dived in front of me. Staring only at the murky water and trying to pretend that I was anywhere else.

These people weren't familiar with tourists or campers, who would want to vacation in a small village who's redeeming feature was a duckpond? I thought this as I watched the algae green water swirl in the middle as a small fish gulped at the surface. It was true that the landscape was indeed beautiful and I could see people travelling South for that, but surely they would be more inclined to visit the tourist hotspots rather than a random, tired village close to Bodmin. Besides a couple of rooms above the pub, I had not seen another hotel or B&B. It was very apparent that tourists were not encouraged nor welcomed.

As I sat on that bench by the pond and chewed monotonously on a sausage roll, I further felt the bubbling of bile. The crippling anxiety that I just couldn't seem to shake. We all have an inner intuition. I'm not just talking about someone talking behind your back this time, this was something deeper and serious. At the time, I just couldn't put my finger on what it was. When the villagers looked at me, they looked at me like they hated me. Like I was meat that they were getting ready to cover with pastry and serve up in their weird bakery. Mountmend existed under a shroud of grey clouds, ominous in its very nature.

Everywhere I looked it was like I was in a parallel universe. I wish that I could bring the feeling up and transfer it to you telepathically, you would hate it. You would want to be rid of it.

I mentioned before that Conan was a bit of a hoarder. Well, it was the same everywhere in his house. You opened a cupboard, and it was filled with books and folders where there shouldn't be books and folders. I found a stack of calendars from every year since 1999. Tom hadn't even attempted to go up into the loft just yet, and him and Arthur had barely made any progress since they had stayed up until 3am trying to get as much packed away as possible. Arthur had since gone home to shower and sleep, and Tom and I were left sifting through piles of paperwork and separating them into "keep" and "shred".
I took myself into Conan's room with an empty box. If anything, I was curious about him. I was drawn to this mysterious hoarder, someone who Lena had said was such a staple in the community. A community that felt perplexing. I wondered how he fit in.

Conan was an artist who lived in the solitude of this big house, taking his inspiration from the illustrious grounds that he was lucky enough to live amongst. It was almost poetic. I found it more alluring than the view I have here in Fullingham, as the woods oozed an air of mystery instead of entrapment. His paintings certainly captured that. They had been stacked up under a tarpaulin in the shed. They were just as you would expect, oil landscapes. Winter, Summer, Autumn, Spring. He painted his backyard in the seasons, a scary reminder of the fluidity of time.

His bed was made neatly, against a red back wall with a large black and white painting hanging in the centre. The oak bed-frame was ornate and looked expensive, intricately carved ivy gave the frame an opulent feel as it twisted up from the feet to the oval tipped bedposts. Directly opposite the bed was a dark oak desk covered in small chips and blemishes. The only other pieces of furniture that completed the room were a cabinet of the same matching wood and a small chair with dusty, dated floral upholstery. I was surprised at the amount of light pouring in from the window behind the desk. I don't know why I expected the room to be shrouded in darkness to reflect the loss of life, but the sun did illuminate the floating dust in sharp, cascading rays.

Out of the window I could see for miles. The hills were covered with trees that stretched and stretched and then descended the other side. The swooping ascent and descent of the hillsides made for an area of outstanding natural beauty. I tried to imagine what it would be like to wake up to this every day, to not stare out of the window at the wheelie bins and a beaten-up old Mazda. Guildford was full of bustle, whereas Mountmend was full of a different kind of life. It was sort of refreshing to me.

I put the box on the floor next to me and started opening the desk drawers. Pulling out papers and casting them in the box to take to the shredder. I came across the typical elements you'd find in the writing desk of a male born in the late 1920s. A Parker jotter ballpoint pen that was difficult to twist, a pack of Christmas cards with black and white snow-covered huts on the front, and in the top right drawer was a plethora of random business cards and takeaway menus.

In the bottom left drawer, I encountered a brown leather box with painted vines across the lid. It was the size of a small treasure chest with a faded brass clasp. I assumed immediately that this was Conan's ex-wife's due to the intricate detail that reminded me of a jewellery box. In the bottom drawer of his desk and right at the back, it could only be something that he didn't get out very often. It smelt like musk.

I carefully undid the clasp and opened the box to find a selection of black and white photos and newspaper clippings. The photos were group shots, smiling faces and arms thrown casually around each other's shoulders. I could make out Arthur on the left and Mr Ward in the middle. In another I saw the Baker from the village. Arthur and Clement Ward were years younger, sporting youthful faces and slicked back hair with trousers up to their armpits. Men and women, together in front of the church and another in front of a fire pit. It felt like I was looking at something staged, something from a film. Who took the photo? Who suggested that they stand like that and who said "smile" when the camera clicked? Conan was clearly popular and a staple in amongst his peers, taking centre stage of every shot like he was the father of a large family and this portrait was going to be hung in the hallway or adorn the front of a Christmas card. I rubbed at the newspaper clippings between my fingers. There were some stories about an annual flower show, another where Conan had won a prize for his geraniums. I read another about a painting of his that depicted the hillside views from his garden that he had sold to raise money for a local charity. Reading that, I immediately built up a picture of Conan that made him into a righteous and charitable man. He was a kind older gentleman who was talented and couldn't bear to get rid of anything due to the sentimental value. It was tame, comfortable.

The last clipping I encountered was different than the others. It was from 4 years prior. The picture was a black and white smiling little boy with tousled blonde hair and smart dungarees. The headline jumped out at me in bold black ink:

Search Continues for Missing Mountmend Boy

I read about 8-year-old Rowan Wearne and how he disappeared suddenly, straight out of his front garden. His Mother had asked him to wait with the dog whilst she ran in for something and had found him vanished upon her return. All that was left of him was the dog. The report was robotic, as you're probably used to. Devoid of emotion and just reporting the hard facts. This young boy had been into boats and had been part of the scouts. A lump formed in my throat.

A similar thing had happened back in Guildford, a young girl went missing from a busy park in the centre of town. They found her a day later wandering along the reservoir, dehydrated and crying for her Mother. Children don't just vanish in a place like Mountmend, where everyone knows everyone, and everyone suspects everyone. The article suggested that there were no leads, and that instead they were just scouring the forest every day on the assumption that he had taken off up there somewhere. It was hard for a village of that size to comprehend that anything sinister had happened to him at all, and that someone that they had known all their lives had been capable of doing it. I sighed. An explanation for why they all hated visitors so much. They may have suspected that an outsider was responsible for Rowan's disappearance. Not one of their own.

What I struggled to comprehend, was why Conan had this in his desk. Why was it hidden away in a box mixed with news articles about his successes and village life? I folded the newspaper article back up and stuffed it into my back pocket, ready to ask Tom about this article that was tugging at my empathies and making me feel uncomfortable.

"Where did you get that?" He was hunched over the stove stirring a tinned soup. He scowled. I held the newspaper clipping out in front of him.

"His bedroom," I stuttered, "Conan's."

He stepped towards me and pulled the newspaper from my grip, scanning it intently.

"I do remember this," Tom said, "But it's nothing. The Wearne Family were family friends, my Grandad was fond of his father. They still live in the village."

"The boy?"

"Yes," Tom chucked the newspaper article nonchalantly into the shred pile on the dining table, "Everyone thinks the father did something to Rowan, he's just weird. But Grandad didn't think that."

"What did he think happened?"

"I don't know, Polly," Tom sighed, "It's been 4 years, he's gone."

I found that rather cold and I scowled back. Tom didn't flinch at all and continued to stir with a limp wrist and minimal effort. It did sort of explain why Conan had the article, if the Wearne family had been close friends of his. Tom's frostiness to situations was something that bothered me every time he expressed it. I was always uneasy as to how quickly he would switch from outstanding joy for a happy couple that he was photographing as they tied the knot to an aloofness at a recent atrocity on the news. He was able to switch off when I couldn't, distance himself. I would sometimes get emotional, and he would tell me how silly I was being. I learnt, being with Tom, that I needed to suppress my emotions just as he did. My Mother hated it. She said that I had become almost robotic. I had to remind her that I still felt these things, I just didn't outwardly express them. They would certainly return in the form of vomit or tears when I was holding in too much.

I picked at a loose thread hanging from my flannel shirt, I didn't want to push and there was something about Tom that closed itself off from interfering. He clammed up so much that you didn't want to waste your energy prying him open again.
I went for it anyway, "They didn't find a body?"
Tom sighed, "No. They didn't. I told you though, they have no leads, he's gone."
I was experiencing all these feelings that I was struggling to name. I took it for the fact that a man had just died in that house, and I was staying somewhere that was completely unfamiliar to me and acting like it was mine. It

did feel uncomfortable. I felt overwhelmed by it all. I couldn't make sense of the newspaper and I felt terrible for the mother of that boy. I still see his face now, smiling up at me immortalised in black and white.

Tom said I was flustered and starting to grate on him. I was grating on myself too, truth be told. He shipped me off to Lena's to have a cup of tea and keep her company.

She did try to pretend that she didn't think that her brother had just parred me off on her, and she acted as hospitable as she usually did. The house was just as pristine as it was when I'd first seen it. I waited for my tea and fingered at the ring of vines sat curiously on top of the mantel piece. It looked like a peculiar ornament, one that should be hung on the wall and not displayed stood up against the wall. It was the size of a small plate and looked handmade. Every time I went into Lena's living room I was drawn to it. I wanted to take it home. Lena cleared her throat and I jumped, "Sorry, I was just admiring your photos."
She placed the tea down on a cork coaster on the coffee table,

"The sandpit, that was at Maggie's house just over the way there."

"Is it weird?" I asked, "Not leaving here? Tom moved away."

She fell back onto the sofa and crossed one leg daintily over the other, "No. I mean, I grew up here, and I got married here. Tom didn't have any ties. When I got married, I think he felt like he needed to do something significant too."

I nodded, "How old were you when you married Arthur?"

"20." Lena recalled. Her eyes seemed to gloss a bit as she sipped her tea. I was 24, and I wasn't even ready to marry Tom yet. At 20 I was at the pub and then subsequently the local bar with Jade, dancing and cheering and then vomiting outside the kebab shop further up the street. I was still living at home with my Mum, having my washing done for me and spending all my money on online shopping. I couldn't imagine putting on a white dress and saying I do to a man who was old enough to be my father.

I smiled as best I could, but Lena read my thoughts and sighed, "I know what you're thinking, and it wasn't like it wasn't thought out. Grandad, he introduced us and then it just…developed."

"I wasn't thinking that," I garbled, "I was just thinking that he seems very nice."

"Arthur? Yeah, he is."

"Older… though." I couldn't help myself.

She chuckled, her laugh dripping with what seemed to me like resentment, "He is. But he was a plumber and had a good salary and he's funny too."

Was she convincing me? Or herself?

I smiled, raising my eyebrows like I was pleasantly impressed.

Lena was the same age as Tom by now, so had been with Arthur 8 years by this point. No children. Her house was pristine, and she seemed to be by herself a lot. I watched her intently as she spoke and I did get the premonition that all was not as it seemed, but I seemed to be getting that jittery feeling a lot lately, so I just squashed it downwards and told myself not to trust it.

4

If you take the time to have nothing to do, you will quickly see that you had previously been buffering away your days with useless hobbies and paraphernalia. There was only so many times within a week I could watch reruns of Last of The Summer Wine and eat salted popcorn from a plastic bowl. When I wasn't doing that, I was helping Tom clear as much as possible and slowly things were being shredded or transported to the tip. Others were taken to Lena's, and others were being sold through auctions or eBay. I would gaze from the living room window and watch Arthur drive away, his backseat full to the brim with trinkets.

The funeral was arranged for the following week, and Tom finalised the details with the funeral directors. My Mother called on the Sunday Morning.
"How are you getting on? Will you be back for next week?" She asked.
 It was my birthday the following Sunday. The day Spring turns to Summer.
"I don't think so, Mum, I'm sorry. The Funeral is Tuesday, I need to wait until Tom's ready to go."
"Could you not get the train? We are supposed to be going to that new Japanese restaurant and I've been wanting to go for ages."
"Mum, it's a tiny village in the middle of nowhere. The nearest train station is somewhere near Bodmin." I also didn't want to come home because I didn't want to go back to work, but that was incredibly selfish of me at the time, and I would absolutely jump at that opportunity if it was presented to me now. Hindsight is a funny thing.
"Ok, ok, we'll have to go when you're back though."
I laughed and agreed.
"How is it down there?" Mum asked, "What's it like?"
"Um, quiet. There's not much to do."
"What's Tom's Sister like?"
"Lena? Fine. Really nice."

"Okay," There was an awkward pause, "Please call me in the week. Give my love to Tom."
I said that I would, and she was gone.

My Mother was a funny woman. I grew up surrounded by books and loose paperwork, mountains of essays and documents that spread like a fungus from her office into our lounge. My friends would say she was eccentric, but I would say that she was smart and loving. My Mum and I had a great time, and I didn't really feel the absence of a father figure because I didn't experience ever having one in the first place. Mum didn't date either, she always said she was too busy and instead just spent her time attending plays and drinking port with her 2 friends. She seemed happy enough where she sat in life. I looked at that and thought that was what I wanted too.

By the evening on that Sunday, Tom announced that he was off out.

The sun was beginning to set, and the sky was a thick orange hue that was quickly seeping into a lustrous, bright red. I thought at first that he was going to the local pub where he had told me that him and his old school friends

used to frequent every Friday and Saturday night, but when I questioned it, he said that he was going down to the village to meet a friend.
"Well, who is it?" I asked.
"An old friend, from school."
He didn't pick up the car keys.
"Are you walking?"
"Yes."
"But you don't like walking."
"Polly, I've just come back to the countryside where I grew up after years of living in the suburbs. I want to go for a walk." He barked.
I sunk into the sofa. I could see him in the doorway struggling with his shoes.
"See you later?" I tried.
"Yep. See you." He said, and the door clicked shut.
I hopped up almost immediately and paced for a while. I didn't know who Tom was meeting, and I did wonder if this "friend" was a woman and he didn't want me to know. I had only once in our entire relationship exhibited a jealous rage, and that was when Leo showed me some pictures of a recent wedding they had shot, and Tom was in the background of one of them with his arms around the waist of a wedding guest. Her arms were around his

neck, like they were locked in a slow dance from the 80s.
He was smiling and she was looking up into his eyes. He
denied anything happened, of course. Tom said that she
was a perspective client who was engaged, and he was
trying to make a good impression, and that I was
overreacting. He made me feel crazy enough that I just let
it go, and I shut up after that about a lot of things.

I went to the cupboards in the kitchen and opened them
one by one. Most were empty now that Tom had been at
the contents. Some were filled with our own bits and
pieces like tea, coffee and cans of soup and spaghetti
hoops. I opened a strange little corner
cupboard and found it filled with wine. I pulled one out
and it was a merlot, exactly what I had been looking for.
I only had a mug, so I figured that was as good as
anything.
I don't remember much of what happened that evening
after I had finished my second mug of wine. I helped
myself to a barrel of crisps, I know that much because I
found the remnants of a large packet and crumbs
scattered across the sofa and carpet. I must have fallen
asleep right where I was sat, because I did have a vague
memory of Tom's blurry face carrying me up the stairs to

bed. I think he asked what on earth I was doing. Usually, it was the other way round and I was the one having to carry Tom through to the bedroom whilst he whispered some obscenities in my ear.

Around 5am, I awoke naturally. It was starting to light up and the room was no longer pitch dark, it was shadier. My head pounded with the weight of a full bottle of red wine, my throat itched, and I could feel the start of indigestion fizz in my stomach. I rolled over onto my back and felt for Tom who dozed beside me. That was the best night's sleep I had in weeks, and I still managed to wake up early and not be able to sleep again. Instead, I pulled myself out of bed in the search of a glass of water. I stepped towards the window and pulled the curtain back slightly, yawning and scratching at the itch the bedsheets had created.
I was right, it was getting light out but very slowly. I could see birds flittering around the trees next to the shed. Some of them were chittering too.
Out of the corner of my eye, I saw a chimney of thick grey smoke billowing upwards towards the sky. It was streamlined, shooting upwards and then dissipating into the atmosphere. It reminded me of a fire on a desert island, an SOS call. I considered for a moment its

placement. The surrounding trees providing a live trail of ignition materials. Cortisol pumped through my veins as I was reminded of news bulletins with pictures of roaring fires spreading through the wilderness. *Who was out in the forest at this time of night? Was it hot enough for wildfires to ignite?* Panic surged through me. I dropped the curtain and ran over to Tom, leaping on top of him and shaking his shoulder.

"Tom!" I tried, "Tom!"

He stirred, groaning.

"Tom, there's a fire!"

He rolled onto his back, sniffing, "What?"

"There's a fire. We need to call somebody."

He eventually opened his eyes and considered me for a moment, "What are you talking about?"

I jumped up and ran to the curtain, pulling it back. "See? The smoke!"

He reluctantly threw back the covers and headed towards me, peering out the window through squinted eyes.

I looked at him expectantly.

He swallowed, "Oh, that. That's nothing. It's fine."

I was taken aback by his response, "What?"

He started back to bed, shuffling along the carpet like his legs no longer worked, "Forget it, Polly. It's just a fire that someone has put out and it's still simmering."

It didn't look like the simmering embers of a fire. It streamed upwards with all the thickness and ferocity of a fire that still raged.

"Do people...do that a lot? In the forest?"

"I don't know, Polly! It's 5am!" He covered his head with the duvet and wiggled further into the mattress. He was no longer receptive of my questions.

I looked back outside at the smoke, twisting its way through the trees and into the skyline. I became evermore curious. I took a deep breath and tried to release the intensity of my clenching muscles in my chest. A fire, in the woods. There was something dangerous about the woods. As the trees stared back at me they seemed to pulse in my vision, fuzzy around the edges. It is the last thing that you expect to see, especially at 5am. I considered that I wasn't in the city anymore and the area was dotted with local farms who may need to be lighting fires at this time in the morning. Garden waste or something. I was also hinting to myself that I might just be bored and wanted something to think about that would take my mind off my raging hangover. It was easier to think that.

I did not expect, in the lead up to my birthday, that I would be away from home and attending the funeral of a man I had never met. Conan was still a bit of a mystery to me, and I was hoping that maybe the eulogy would shed some light on how this man had grown up and what his life was like before he adopted Tom and Lena. His house only indicated so much, I had no idea of any of the struggles or successes besides from his Geraniums and the pictures of his village friends. No, I hadn't been into his bedroom since that day I found the newspaper clipping. That was thrown into the shredder with Tom's haste, but as I stood in the mirror in the bathroom pulling at the high neck on my black dress, I wondered if they had a funeral for Rowan Wearne. If his mother had buried an empty casket like they do when the bodies are lost at sea. Did she still hold out hope that he would come home to her? Or did his headstone sit amongst the others in the village cemetery?

It rained on that Tuesday morning when the funeral was to take place, just like it had on the night we had found out that Conan had died. It hammered, and I was pleased that I'd found an umbrella in the cupboard in the hallway. Just like my dress it was a mournful black. Some insane kind of pathetic fallacy, it always rained on the darkest days. Tom was waiting for me at the bottom of the stairs, pulling up his white socks in a stark contrast to his dark chequered suit trousers and black blazer. He looked good suited up. It reminded me of the day we first met.

We drove, we didn't walk. As we passed through the village, we drove through a steady stream of umbrellas as people walked towards the church. It was a whole village affair. A sea of black umbrellas bobbed up and down as people spilled into the road through onto Church Lane.

I turned to Tom, "A good turn out, then?"

Tom sighed, "I used to go to church every Sunday, Grandad used to take me and make me shake the hands of everyone in the village as they were leaving. Everyone used to pile into the pub after for a roast dinner. I was allowed one glass of coke and then Grandad would give me a sip of his cider, it was always dry and sour."

I swallowed. Tom spilt more than I had expected, and the words hung in the air of the humid car as I took them in. It was the first snippet of an anecdote that involved Tom within his Grandad's life on a personal level. The church had been important in his memory, connected him to Conan. Travelling towards that church for Conan's final commitment had opened a void of vulnerability in Tom. I could see it as he blinked, eyes fixed ahead as the rain pummelled the windscreen and was thrown off by the wipers with a wet flourish. We pulled into the small car park just as I was about to respond, but before I could open my mouth Tom had jumped from the car and slammed the door behind him.

 The church was exactly what I expected, and probably what *you* would expect of a village church. It was small and grey with one big, arched stained-glass window at the back. The building itself was enveloped by trees and looked ominous in the pouring rain as it turned the stone from a soft grey into a dark-coloured mortar. The ground squelched as we crossed the grass and made it to the path leading to the front door. I tried to stick to the path to save my shoes from the mud. Nobody spoke, and Tom just received the occasional shoulder squeeze or comforting pat on the back as they parted ways to let us pass. It was eerily silent, not even the sound of an organ echoing through open space. The silence itself was almost deafening and I tried to ignore how clammy my hands felt as I squeezed them into fists at my side. Clement Ward stood in the arched doorway, shaking hands with everyone who passed through. His hair was neatly gelled without a single strand out of place. He took Tom's hand and shook it gently.

"Hello, Thomas," Clement's brows were furrowed in concern, "How are you holding up?"

Tom sighed, "I'm okay. Is Lena here?"

Clement gestured to the front where Lena was sat with Arthur whispering with a thin woman wearing a black fascinator.

Clement smiled at me as I walked past, a soft smile that made the hairs on my neck raise. I find it hard to describe him to you, because his disposition was so unique that I couldn't quite put my finger on what made him that way. His mouth was a thin line like the lips of a reptile and were just as scaly. He towered over everyone with his shoulders hunched and his head jutted. At this time, I knew practically nothing about him or his wife, except his obvious role as the pastor. Everyone in the village knew his name and shook his hand as if they admired his very being alive. He seemed to float without ridiculous fanfare amongst his peers, offering words of comfort and advice. I had seen these types of men before. The type who everyone holds in such a high regard only for them to fall spectacularly when something inevitably scandalous was to emerge. He walked like they walked, like he was

invincible.
We took a seat next to Lena whose mascara had already smudged slightly around the outer corners of her eyes. She had a fistful of crumpled tissue in one hand. Arthur touched her knee tentatively, but she didn't react, only continued to sniffle and gaze with longing at the stained glass which was darkened and less vibrant against the grey sky.
I had only ever been to one funeral before. My Grandad. I was only 6 so I don't really remember much of what happened during the actual ceremony, I just had a vivid memory of his coffin lowering into the ground and my mother crying so much that her eyes were so swollen that you couldn't even see them anymore. He was placed into the dark, rectangular hole in the ground, and I had to throw a singular rose on top of him. I struggled to believe that my Grandad was in that box, in the cold ground, and that we were standing there looking at the place where he would be buried for centuries to come. People sniffed and sobbed around me. It was my first glimpse at something so sinister, so real.
Conan's eulogy didn't reveal as much as I'd hoped it would, but it did give me a slither of a glimpse into his life. His wife had been Joanne, it was not mentioned where she

was now or why they separated. I glanced around the church to see if there was a reaction from any of the older ladies at the mention of her name. I went to nudge Tom and ask him, but he looked deep in thought, and it didn't feel appropriate. I still don't know much about Tom's Grandmother. No amount of research has told me anything, in fact its lead me to believe that she died a long time ago. Conan had been a pastor himself and was apparently a huge favourite amongst the villagers. He was a keen painter and horticulturist. Tom and Lena's father was briefly mentioned as Conan's only child, gone too soon in the wreckage of a car accident close by. Then onto Lena and Tom, described as his own children in everything but biology. Clement described how Conan had raised them. He took them to church on a Sunday, to book fairs, to school dances and to the seaside on the hottest day of the year. I looked at Lena then. Her nose was scrunched up and mouth downturned in an effort to control her quiet sobbing, tears rolled slowly down her cheeks. Tom's face remained blank.
A hymn was sung. I didn't really know the words, so I just mouthed them as best I could. Clement wrapped up with a prayer and a blessing, bowing his head at Conan's coffin before making his was down the aisle towards the back

doors. Pallbearers in their sleek black suits balanced the coffin upon their shoulders and followed Clement out. The congregation stood and watched him go.
I wasn't sure what we were supposed to do, so I followed closely behind Tom as he made his way into the cemetery. People funnelled out with umbrellas hoisted high to weave through people. Lena was ahead of us being guided by Arthur's arm around her shoulders.
A plot was already dug. The outskirts were covered in a green tarpaulin and wooden slats holding his coffin above the ground. I did feel a sense of familiarity as we came to the edge of the hole, staring at the wooden structure that contained something that I found difficult to fathom. It forced me to consider my own mortality.

Clement began his final reading, having to project his voice over the sounds of rain slapping against the tarpaulin. The pallbearers had disappeared, just funeral goers and Clement remained. I looked around me. A dozen or more eyes bore into my skin. Everybody at that funeral had eyes on me. I gasped a little, turning back to face the plot and squeezing my eyes shut. I told myself that I was being paranoid, inflicting myself on a private moment that I had no business being a part of. The ground felt like it was starting to swallow me up and soon I'd be underneath the surface amongst the skeletons.

He said it. Ashes to ashes and dust to dust. The pallbearers still didn't appear.

I waited patiently for things to move on, but people suddenly started to leave. The coffin wasn't lowered, it stayed exactly where it was.

I pulled on Tom's arm gently, "Is he not…going in?"

Tom scoffed, "That's not how it's done here, Polly."

"Not how it's done?"

He ignored me, greeting people and shaking their hands, inviting them to the pub for sandwiches. His smile was warm, yet melancholy. Forever a mask. These people took his hand in his and addressed him like he was their own child. I was unfamiliar with the familiarity of people who had lived amongst each other's generations and formed these attachments.

I stood there like a spare part. Looks were shot my way. I couldn't help but glance back at Conan's coffin, sitting atop the wooden slats like the whole thing was over but not quite. Like it was right on the cusp or the tip of your tongue. It felt unfinished. It felt odd.

Tom was calling my name from the gate, and I scuppered after him. If I looked over my shoulder one more time, maybe he would be in the ground. I looked; he was still where he was. In the box upon the slats.
Everything was very concerning to me. I could squash this feeling down like a thought I didn't want to think, cage it in the back of my mind, throw away the key and pretend that everything was fine. These people were grieving a huge loss in their community, and grief can do funny things to people. The voice of reason that I had learnt to trust with every case I worked on.

I told myself it was all normal. Sadly, it all changed when I finally met Mrs Wearne.

5

I didn't stay very long at the wake. It was held in the stale bar area of The Swan, with its distressed and sticky carpet and its bar stained with syrupy rings from beers past. With every step I took it felt like the eyes from the old photos hung on the wall were following me. In amongst the stained drips of mould were framed tickets and letters. One looked like an old steam locomotive ticket, but there were no stations in Mountmend. People flittered and dodged each other to get to the bar. I felt sick and asked Arthur to drive me home. I didn't fancy being further stared at or whispered about, so I decided to leave pretty

much straight away. Tom said that he would bring me home some sandwiches and sausage rolls.
He did bring those back, along with a load of egg sandwiches that I found in the fridge the next morning. I knew my mum would object, but I had them for breakfast.
Truth be told, at this point we were beginning to run out of food and a trip to the supermarket was needed. Tom was still sound asleep when I had finished eating, so I took an old drawstring backpack from the coat rack by Conan's front door and pulled my boots on. I knew a walk would do me good, clear my head, and I could stop at Lena's and see if she would drive me out of town to the supermarket. I made a mental note of what was missing, and toiletries that I was starting to run out of. I recounted this in my head as I took to the gravel and through the opening in the trees.

The drive was winding, and the walk took me along the stone wall of a bright yellow field. I could have taken the car and whizzed round the bends, taking the wrong turns and breathing in the country air through a small gap in the window. I preferred it this way. The meandering walk was full of small flies and the smell of cow shit, but at least

I was seeing some greenery. I used to walk the length of the park in Reigate, stopping at the coffee kiosk to grab a cup of tea before taking the long route back to the flat. I used to do this on Sundays. Tom would be busy editing and there would be not much else to occupy my time. The long walk into the village reminded me of that, and I found myself pulled back into my familiar and secure world at home. Everything in Mountmend felt alien. The traffic started to pick up and the sign to Mountmend Village popped up in front of me.

When I got to the top of the row of small shops, I made a beeline for the green and pushed on towards Lena's house. It was a Thursday, and all was quiet. A gaggle of older women with walking sticks and coloured rain macs emerged from the door of the bakery. A man on a bike whizzed past almost knocking me over. It was the picture of a perfect village, something from an old film. I half expected to see a penny farthing and an old, ornate stroller being pushed by a maid in a white bonnet and a sleek black overcoat. Stuck in the past.

As I was walking, I heard the sound of raised voices coming from Church Lane. The sound carried as if it was being transported on the light breeze. I turned my head to see the familiar tall frame of Clement Ward, his hands nervously wringing together in front of him. A smaller woman in a Barbour coat and a neckerchief was waving her arms about in front of him chaotically.

"…you have no idea what I went through!" The woman roared, her hand was flat against her chest now in dismay.

"Moira, please."

"You should be ashamed of yourself, swanning around here in God's uniform acting like a saint!"

"Keep your voice down." Clement hissed. His face was turning into a particularly poignant shade of tomato. Before I even knew what I was doing, the direction of my feet had changed, and I found myself walking towards the arguing pair. Although I was training to be a solicitor, I'm not one to get into unnecessary conflict. My conflicts are to be well thought out, articulated, and with a clear structure. All the shouting, screaming and scratching made me feel uncomfortable. I'd happily watch a bar fight from the outside and anticipate the laws they are breaking but you wouldn't catch me in the middle, palms on their chests trying to keep them apart. Even in here, in Fullingham, I carry on eating my cornflakes when someone flips a table or stamps on someone else's foot. I felt like it was a bad idea, to intervene here, and I didn't even recognise myself as I was striding over to them. There was something uncomfortable about Clement that made me want to help this poor woman out. It was like my brain hadn't caught up with my legs yet. So uncanny to me, I started to wonder what Mountmend was doing to me.

They didn't notice my approach.

"…Is everything okay? Would you like me to call somebody?" I aimed the question at the woman, Moira, who spun to face me.
"And who on earth are you?"
"Moira, leave Polly out of this." Clement placed a warning hand on her shoulder. She shrugged him off. His utterance of my name made me shiver.
She took a step towards me, until our faces were inches apart. Her skin looked as if it had been battered by the burden of life, with deep-set wrinkles and red rings around her eyes.
"You would leave now if you knew what was good for you." She whispered.
I swallowed, "What?"
"You heard me. Get gone."

I was taken aback by her statement. The ferocity in her eyes. I was sure that my face had drained all colour as I stood staring at her, not sure how to respond. I felt like I'd been blighted by an old witch. Clement looked just as shocked as I was. It added to the swells in the pit of my stomach, made worse by the fact that I looked to my left and realised that pretty much the entire village was watching us. Someone was even hanging from a window, hand cupped to their ear like it was a daytime show.
"Now, now," Clement chuckled, "That's enough."
"Fuck you!"
Moira straightened her jacket, and with a stern look at Clement one more time, she stalked off across the green. I was still frozen in my spot, like I had cement in my shoes. I looked at Clement Ward with an eyebrow raised. Weirdly, he was smiling. He was all lips and no teeth.
"Polly," He sighed, "Please excuse Mrs Wearne. She has, had a lot going on these past few years."
Mrs Wearne. A lightbulb flickered on in my head. She was the worried Mother whose son had disappeared, little Rowan Wearne. Suddenly, her anger and animosity at life had made sense to me. She was fearful of me, an outsider, because she still didn't know what had happened to her son and now she couldn't trust anybody.

"I, er," I cleared my throat, "It's okay. I'm okay."
Clement looked unconvinced, "Just a little disagreement is all, I'm sure you can understand in a small village, we can get under each other's skin sometimes."
"Yes," I pointed over my shoulder, "I'm going to go to Lena's now."
"Of course, of course, if you're sure you okay. Please. Ignore her. She meant no harm."
His attempt at damage control was fruitless, because the damage was already done. I was visibly shaken. Thoughts raced around in my head, and I struggled to focus on anything other than the buzzing in my brain. The feeling of nervousness seemed to have a grip on my throat. I felt Clement's eyes burn into my back as I walked away. Something was amiss. Mrs Wearne clearly felt the same unnerving aura from Clement Ward. She told him that he should be ashamed of himself. A bold statement, but for what? I was skulking around Mountmend with more questions than I had answers. I attempted to pick up the pace to Lena's.

She did take me to the supermarket to pick up some food, but not without asking me multiple times what was wrong and if I was okay. As much as I tried to stop wiping at the sweat on the back on my neck and picking at the skin around my nail, it was obvious. I said I was fine, and that I was just tired. She confessed that she was also tired as Arthur had come home from the wake yesterday a bit too drunk and kept her up with his snoring. I resisted the urge to again ask why she married him when she spoke about him with such disdain, but I knew it wasn't really any of my business. Every time she said his name, her expression was close to a grimace. It was as hard to believe that Lena was some kind of gold-digger. I watched her cling to comfort like I used to. It wasn't until I was thrust out of it that realised how much I missed it, but also how much I didn't miss it at all. Fullingham is a different kind of comfort. I couldn't remember what life was like on the outside. Inside I had safety.

I couldn't shake that electric feeling that I felt after the argument in the village. Even after Lena had dropped me off and dinner was cooked and eaten, I still felt a tightness in my chest and an unsettling nausea in my stomach. I just wanted to shut myself away, but ideally, I wanted to shut myself away in my flat in Guildford on the sofa with a blanket, some chocolate and the television. Everything in Mountmend still felt unnervingly unfamiliar. Even Tom.

He barely spoke to me at all. He kept me at arm's length, not even realising that I was out of sorts. He didn't ask where I'd been that day or who I had spoken to. He didn't ask who dropped me off. He *did* ask me if I'd bought more eggs.

If I'm honest, my patience for his increasing distance from me was starting to waiver. I was trying to remember that the man had just lost the only father figure he had in his life, but I was also resenting the fact that he wasn't confiding in me and therefore I felt uncomfortable confiding in him anymore. His mood rubbed off on me and I oftentimes found myself swimming in the same pool of misery just because he was. It didn't start off that way with us, but it developed into a situation where I was trying to lift him up all the time. His work wasn't good enough, his flat wasn't good enough, his friends had abandoned him, and the rent was going up in his studio space. Every day there was a new complaint that left him reeling and unhappy. I didn't ask anymore. When I got home from work, dinner was cooked and eaten with barely a word said between us. The sofa sunk in the middle where we both sat night after night. The TV illuminated a dark living room with continuous boring re-runs. I had already begun to back away from him, so imagine how surprised I was when he proposed to me. He fell on one knee on a rolling white beach on the coast of Mexico, after I'd spent much of the holiday on a sun lounger reading lifestyle magazines whilst Tom could barely sit still. He spent hours photographing locals sitting on dusty doorsteps and drinking copious amounts of tequila at the beach bar. By the time dinner rolled round he stunk of alcohol and his proposal was slurred, but I couldn't fault the romanticism that I used to devour so much. I would have done anything to be living in the plot of a chick flick. Those love stories are mostly written by women.

Despite all of the mess, I loved Tom. I wouldn't have said yes if I didn't. I couldn't leave him when he needed me so much. It is weird how much self-sacrifice goes into being with someone, isn't it?

That night, I didn't want to go to bed. Tom went up relatively early with a yawn and a short "night". I stayed up longer watching some old black and white film on the TV, with a cup of tea and a punnet of grapes. I was illuminated by only one small lamp shaped like a duck and the flickering glow of the television which occasionally glitched. The curtains to the living room were closed, but I noticed that Tom had left the ones in the kitchen open. It made me nervous, in the middle of nowhere with the curtains wide open, a sea of pitch black as far as you could see. I took myself into the kitchen with the notion of shutting them.

As I rounded the table, one of the movement sensing outside lights by the back door flickered to life, and I stopped in my tracks.

My breath immediately sped up, but a part of my mind rationalised that it was probably just a fox or a rabbit or something. This was a farmhouse in the middle of the countryside. I screwed my nose up at any mention in my brain of the "beast of Bodmin". Pure fairy-tale.

I took another step, but again I was halted. Underneath the lit gap at the bottom of the back door was the dancing movement of a shadow, a black shadow that moved as if whatever it was was standing right in front of the door just metres away from me. It moved for a moment, then stopped still, and I felt a prickly sensation in the back of my neck. Like I was being watched.

I was very conscious of the ferocity of my breathing. I went to call for Tom, but my mouth was dry and sticky. All I could hear was the pounding of my pulse loud in my

ears. There was nobody in the glass. No outline or hint of colour. If this was the case, why did the shadow, this *stationary* shadow, appear to have broad shoulders and the strong outline of a head.
I hesitated. My bare feet glued to the cold kitchen tiles. I could feel something prickly begin to tickle my skin. I slowly reached for the back of my neck. A faint buzz echoed in my ear, getting louder and louder as I slapped my hand down on my skin. It stopped. Suddenly, a small fly whizzed out from the back of my head and into my vision. Then two. Then three. More and more appeared as the air was sucked from my body. I was frozen. I glanced back at the shadow. I didn't want to move. I tried to flap my arms gently in an attempt to shoo them away. I tried to reason with myself as I stood there swatting at flies and whimpering quietly. My mind buzzed with the same hum of the flap of their wings. I either opened the door and checked whatever it was standing there and faced the consequences should I not like what I found, or I made a break for the stairs and wake Tom up to investigate. The latter won, and as I took my first step back, the automatic light went off and plunged me into a thick darkness.

Tom did come downstairs. I woke him up when I screamed.

You will probably guess that he found nothing. He even did a loop of the outside of the house with an old torch to see if he could see animal tracks. He said it was too far out of the village for anyone to be out walking this late, and therefore it must have been some type of creature running about in the dark. He told me badgers were bigger than I thought.
I knew what I had seen and was not overly convinced by his explanation. As I lay in bed next to Tom, I thought about the shadow again. The way it had moved and stopped stock still, caught in it's tracks by the illumination of the outside light. I was sure that it was a human shadow. My mind could play tricks on me. One late night when I was seven I pushed past bedtime and decided to stay up all night. I was so tired, that I stared up from my bed at a picture of a fluffy bear with a blue bow tie. The longer I stared at it, the more it appeared to move and dance. I called out for my Mum. She stroked my hair and said, "Oh sweetheart, sometimes when you look at things through sleepy eyes they can look a little bit different." I would look up at that bear with the blue bow tie whenever

I was tired and enjoy the little samba it did until I drifted off to sleep. The stress of the funeral made my eyes burn. The strange shadow reminded me of that painting. I rolled over slowly. The back of my neck continued to itch, and as I scratched at it a small lump formed. It was annoyingly itchy.

It became more difficult to dismiss my thoughts the more I contemplated what I'd seen. Do you believe in ghosts, the paranormal? Well, I didn't. I was a lawyer in training, I was all about the facts and figures. The evidence. I had seen this shadow and thought, "that is evidence". There was nothing in the glass of the backdoor to suggest that anyone was there, standing underneath that light, yet the shadow across the kitchen floor was there as plain as day. It almost taunted my rational thoughts, lifted me into a different realm of possibility.

I struggled to fall asleep from the adrenaline that was humming throughout my body, heightened by my thoughts. I tossed and turned and scratched. When I did fall asleep, I fell deeply into a string of nightmares. Not the usual teeth falling out or standing in front of your classmates in just your underwear, but these felt darker and

oozed discomfort. They were dark and vignette around the edges. They were shaky and all consuming.
Within the reels of my dreams was a man. He hovered on the edge of scenarios filled with pain. He was fuzzy like he hadn't quite been tuned correctly. Amongst the ashes of an apocalyptic scene, on the shore whilst the tide came in and my feet were deeply buried in the sand, watching from the window whilst I was being chased down a dimly lit city alleyway. Suddenly, everything stopped. Like a cut scene, I was standing in what appeared to be a dimly lit bedroom. It resembled Conan's old antique furniture & traditional set up. I barely had time to take in my surroundings with any detail. Straight ahead of me was the man from my dreams. The man wore a crinkly, long leather jacket, towering over a woman hunched in the corner with her head in her hands. Streaks of wet blonde hair were shielding the features from her face. He stared down at her; his knuckles white with the intensity of the fist he was making with his hands. The energy that rolled off him was an angry one. It was like heat from a radiator that you can almost see from the right angle. I wanted to help her, but as with many dreams I found myself mute and stilted. He lifted his fist and drew it backwards as she sobbed beneath him. Her body shook with every wail.

I did everything I could. Twitched every muscle until I could lift my foot and take a heavy step forward. The man in the leather jacket flinched, his head flicked to the side like a predator who had just got a whiff of his prey. He turned to face me, but his face was white and misty like it was covered with a thick fog. I could not make out a singular feature. He didn't look human.
This time, his fist was raised at me. I wanted to beg, I wanted to scream, but all I could see was a fist flying towards my face before I woke up covered in sweat.

6

There was something strangely compelling about the little boy who went missing. Rowan Wearne. His Mother was furious at Clement for something that I did not understand, and the way her eyes had glossed over when she was telling me to leave made me even more confused. I didn't want to think about it, the boy who went missing. But I would take this as a welcome distraction from the shapes and shadows from the night before. My throat was permanently tight. I was looking for something that would give me some kind of purpose. I felt more alone than before in Conan's house. I was beginning to question my

own thoughts with what could only be a dangerous ferocity.
I did feel different. I'm struggling to explain it to you. That feeling as if you are being watched and your skin feels itchy, and you can't help but feel for the hairs standing upright on the back of your neck. This felt permanent as I carried forward into the day. Even as I stood in the bathroom mirror brushing my teeth or washing up in the sink. I was checking over my shoulder. I would shake my hands out or roll my neck in an attempt to snap out of it. Whatever I did, I couldn't shake it.

Tom left before I awoke the next morning, texting me to say that he was over at Lena's. I didn't really want to be by myself, but pride prevented me from asking Tom to stick around. He would say I was stupid or silly. He was out more often than he was in whilst we were in Mountmend. He had to speak to persons that I did not know. I understood that being back in your hometown in the midst of a crisis, everybody wanted to be the one to offer their condolences the haoordest. He was flighty and busy.
I was feeling hard done by. A feeling I wasn't unfamiliar with, but one that was equivalent to the feeling of a weight hanging from my neck. As I wandered from room to room

I felt uncomfortable in every one that I stood in. Eventually, I decided to take that familiar path into the village and walk to Lena's house myself. Even if Tom objected, I couldn't be here any longer with the swell of my own thoughts.

When I made it to the village, I kept my head down as I walked across the green towards Lena and Arthur's house. As I was walking down the street towards her recognisably pristine front lawn, I saw a familiar face bringing in her washing from another front garden. It was Mrs Wearne. Her house stood out amongst some of the newer buildings on her street, a small, rickety cottage with a front garden full of rosebushes, iron furniture and a birdbath. It looked like an old ceramic teapot where the pot is the house and the roof is the lid. Her gate was rusted and squeaked lightly in the gentle breeze. I was watching her as she pulled the basket into her arms and went back inside, shutting the door behind her.
I considered the opportunity that had been presented to me. An apt opportunity to give in to my curiosity once and for all. I stopped in my tracks and stared at Mrs Wearne's front door. It was green and the paint was peeling.

My inquisitive nature drew me to a boy who hadn't had the happiest ending and I felt somewhere, deep down, that I would get answers. I wanted to know what her and Clement were arguing about. Maybe I was just nosey. Or bored. Or an innate need to be distracted.
Before I could even tell myself any different, my feet were striding across the road and in through the squeaky gate. The pebbles of the path rustled and crunched beneath the soles of my shoes, alerting those inside the house to a visitor.

I sighed and knocked gently on the door.

I didn't give myself a chance to think at all about what I was doing, and I think that this was the reason that I stuttered when the door opened a slither and a pair of eyes looked up at me.
"Yes?" Mrs Wearne's voice was stern.
"Uh, Hi," I spluttered, "I'm Polly?"
She pulled the door back a bit more so she could take in more of me, her eyebrows knitted together into a frown.
"You're the girl from yesterday. What do you want?"

"Well, look. I was just coming by to see if you were okay. The argument yesterday with Mr Ward looked pretty intense and I just…" I trailed off. My hands were flailing awkwardly, I wasn't sure I sounded entirely convincing. Her expression did soften slightly, but she remained on her guard. Shoulders square and hand firmly grasping the door handle should she need to close it in a hurry.
"What business is it of yours?"
"Well, it isn't, really…" I sighed, "but I was just concerned."
She considered me for a moment more, before slowly pulling the door open and stepping to the side, "You'd better come in, hadn't you?"
I felt overwhelming relief that she hadn't slammed the door in my face, and as I stepped past her and into the hallway, I was aware of the old-fashioned theme that was evidently popular in a lot of the houses around here. It was stuck in the past, standing still where it had been all those years. Mrs Wearne's was an eclectic mixture of eras. A carpet from the 60s, wallpaper from the 70s and a velvety fringed green sofa that was slightly yellowing along the corners. The living room was just off from the front door, and Mrs Wearne gestured to me to take a seat. I sunk into a space on that sofa that had clearly been

burrowed over a number of years. Ahead of me was a big stone fireplace, and next to it a TV that still had the big back.

"Tea?" She asked.

"That would be lovely." I smiled as warmly as I could towards her.

She disappeared into the kitchen, and I could hear the clinking of china. A kettle whistled from the stove. I glanced around. On the mantelpiece sat that same circle of vines that I had seen on Lena's mantlepiece. It was intricate, perhaps a local seller who they knew. It was resting against the back wall and was immediately familiar. Next to it was an abundance of photos in frames and a green bubbled vase with dried daisies in it. Despite the light Spring weather, the curtains were drawn closed. It could have been 9 in the morning or 10 o'clock at night. The room remained the same dusk, amber hue.

Mrs Wearne re-entered carrying a silver tray, adorned with two teacups, a teapot and a plate of thin looking cakes.

She placed this gently on the coffee table and fell back into an armchair, "Roy isn't here at the moment, it's probably for the best. He doesn't really like visitors."

"Thank you." I took the teacup from the tray and rested it gently in my lap.//
"Welsh cake?" She asked, gesturing to the tray full of delectable looking pastries.//
"Sure."//
It tasted sweet and crumbled as I bit into it, like a fruit scone but with a sugary afterthought.//
I licked my fingers as I devoured the last bite, "That was delicious, thank you."//
"Listen, Polly," She leant back, seemingly to relax slightly, "I am sorry that you got caught up in all of that yesterday. I didn't mean to upset you."//
"It's okay, you didn't." I lied.//
"Clement can be difficult. We've never seen eye to eye."//
"Is that because of your son?" I asked. I realised after I asked it that it was probably too intense too quickly.//
Moira Wearne hesitated, "Yes. Partially because of Rowan."//
"Can I ask you about him?"//
"You are aware of what happened I suppose," She sighed, "He was such a bright little boy. He wasn't stupid enough to go off with strangers he didn't know. He was also the apple of his dad's eye, so that isn't the case either, if that's what you're thinking."

"No, no, of course not." I had been.
"He was 8 when he…disappeared. He had so many little friends in the village. He adored it you know, the fields and the forests and the hillsides. He used to collect funny shaped rocks and display them on his bedroom windowsill." She smiled sadly.
"That's lovely, how funny kids can be." Something my Mum had said to a friend. It seemed apt here.
"How funny indeed."
The air was thick with melancholy. Mrs Wearne's expression was faltering, her eyes filling as she remembered her little boy. There was a huge lump in my throat too, hearing her talk about him. It made him real to me as I imagined him running around this living room showing his mother the rocks he found. I suddenly felt terrible for showing up unannounced and forcing her to recount her trauma. Another dangerous liaison for me. I needed to stop getting into these situations.
"Of course, they looked for a while, but they didn't find him." She was definitely starting to unravel. I started to panic as I watched her pick at the hem on her skirt. I shouldn't have asked. I shouldn't have even come in here. I leant forward, trying to show that I was here as a kind

listener. I wasn't ever any good at being a comfort. I rarely knew what to do when people cried.

"Don't lose hope," I tried, "They will find him. I'm sure they will."

She smiled, "You are kind, but damned I'm afraid."

My stomach dropped.

I swallowed, "Pardon?"

"I know what happened to my boy," She started to cry quietly, "I just can't do anything about it."

This was not what I had signed up for. My heart was racing as I hung onto her every word, suddenly realising that my curiosity had come back to bite me like the famous sayings had suggested.

"What do you mean?" I whispered, this time I reached out and took her hands gently in mine. I don't know what was possessing me. I needed to stop pushing.

She sniffled, holding her eyes tightly shut as tears rolled out and down her chin. I patiently waited. She shook her head.

"Mrs Wearne?" I tried.

She took a deep breath and whispered one single word, her eyes wide and locked with mine.

"Pengally."

The door flew open behind us, and Mrs Wearne jumped from her seat with a quickness. She stood back from me, quickly wiping the tears from her eyes.

"Moira?"

It was a man's voice. I turned my head to see a gentleman making his way into the room. He was wearing a tweed flat-cap and a quilted coat. His face was fuzzy with a thick stubble. His skin was weathered.

"In here." She squeaked.

"Who is this?" He asked. He spoke past me, didn't even look in my direction. From where I was sat, I could smell the bitterness of lager. He smelt like a sticky pub.

I looked to Mrs Wearne.

"This is Polly, she's just leaving."

I took that as my queue to stand up, "Thank you for the tea, Mrs Wearne."

I didn't want to go, but the eyes of Mrs Wearne's husband bore into my flesh as I headed to the door.

"Who is she? Not one of those good for nothing psychics again, Moira? They'll swindle you and take your money. They don't care about you and they certainly don't know nothing about Rowan."

His voice was raising. I reached for the handle.

"Roy, please. She's not a psychic."

My impression of Roy was not the best. I did worry what he would say or do when the front door closed behind me. I'd stuck my nose in once, and I didn't want to make matters worse for Mrs Wearne. I took the gravel path with some haste.

I didn't go to Lena's. Instead, I walked back to Conan's.

In hindsight, I could understand Roy Wearne's reaction. He was deeply troubled. Losing a child would surely do that to someone. Worse off is not knowing whether he will ever return, and I could see in just his stance that he was a man on the edge. His life no fuller than the last stool at the corner of the bar, chatting to the older barmaid at the local and wondering if his life would have been different if he'd married her instead.
Despite being ejected from the Wearne's, I kept seeing Moira's terrified face at the forefront of my brain.

"Pengally."

I didn't even know where to begin with this. My head was swimming, a feral mind drama that made it ache and throb. This place where I had ended up was full of things I didn't understand. As I walked home, I felt the tightness within my chest building, and I stopped along the roadside to throw up into a bush. I heaved and heaved until my stomach muscles seemed to cry out for it to stop. I look back now and understand that I was overwhelmed by panic, but at the time I felt like I was being lowered into a well and the pinprick of daylight was getting smaller and smaller the further down I got.

Of course, I had low moods at home, but this was different. Most of us had experienced a profound panic attack. There was something in the air that caught in my throat and made me queasy. It felt like I was inhaling thick farmyard dust.

I couldn't ask Tom about Pengally. I didn't even know if it was a place or a person, friend or foe. But I did know that the name made me shiver slightly at the possibility that whatever it was, it was responsible for Rowan Wearne's disappearance. I did believe Moira. If you had seen the sheer fright within her eyes, you would have believed her too.

Instead, I was in bed by the time Tom got home. He asked me if I wanted soup, but I said I had a migraine. I wasn't exactly lying, because I did feel like my head was pounding with every thought that arose and every new theory that presented itself. I laid there thinking about everything and nothing at once. I squeezed my eyes shut every so often willing the thought carousel to stop, begging it to let me get off. My stomach hurt with every deep breath I took. Before I fell asleep that night, I vowed that I would keep a clearer head.

7

I had anxiety dreams here before they put me on a new type of drug. They feel worry-filled and rushed, like there's a sense of urgency and being out of control. You struggle to find a familiar face amongst your worst fears. Dr Ralph says that the typical dream that hints at anxiety is dreaming that your teeth are falling out. I told her that I hadn't had that one before. Instead, I would dream that I would awake in my bed at Fullingham and there was no one around. The hallways were empty and creepily silent. No squeaking plimsoles or the sound of quiet crying from a shady corner. I would try the doors and they would be sealed tight. In this angst fuelled dream I roamed the hallways shouting for help until my throat was hoarse. At the start of my time at Fullingham, I was having this same dream every night until the haloperidol kicked in.

That was how I felt that night. I knew I was floating adrift from my usual reality. The sense of control slipping through my fingers like sand.
 I saw the man in the leather jacket again that night, standing firm within my dreams again. His face was clearer this time and it was one I did not recognise, and he had a large scar on his right cheek. It looked like it hadn't fully healed and it wept gently. Yellow pus slithered down his cheek like tears. This time he did not approach me. We were both stood staring at each other in the moonlit space of Conan's kitchen. That night he appeared more like a ghost. Pale and fuzzy around the edges. I was still irrevocably afraid of him, and I was trembling and sweating like I had the flu. The look on his face, so serious and spooky, made me uncomfortable. I wish that I could show you what I saw, and you would realise that I had every right to be afraid of him. Even when he was stationary.
A whoosh and I woke up in a cold sweat. I gasped for air, trying my best to regulate my breathing. I could feel the duvet was wet and my hair was stuck to the sides of my

face. My temperature was irregular. The air in the room felt like it was thick with humidity.
"Tom." I whispered.
I felt next to me in the darkness of the bedroom, tapping the bed for any sign of Tom's sleeping body.

He was not there.

I started to panic. "Tom." I said, louder this time. I sat bolt upright. My hand just hit the bed with disturbing thumps, no sign of a body. I pulled back the covers and hopped out of bed. I wondered if he had gone to the bathroom, so I carefully opened the bedroom door and tentatively stepped into the hallway.
"Tom?"
The bathroom door was ajar and the room was shrouded in darkness. It was empty.
A sound. Quick and frightful like a crumpling shoe or squelching leather. My head whipped round to the stairs, where it had come from.
"Tom?" I called into the darkness.
I felt nauseous as I moved towards the stairs, expecting Tom to come bounding up them at any moment and tell me to stop being so stupid and go back to bed.

It was that feeling that comes when you hear a bump in the night, like downstairs is an intruder or an animal that you are going to have to face because there isn't anyone else to do it. It was right in the pit of my stomach, and I wanted to dance on my tiptoes, run on the spot, anything to avoid facing a threat that I could feel in the atmosphere. As my hand touched the wall at the top of the stairs, I peered downwards into a pit of black filled with faint outlines that I could hardly make out.
There was another sound. A faint scuttling that got louder as I breathed. I looked down at my feet.
Hundreds of cockroaches ascended the stairs. The gross smell of dirt caught in the back of my throat as I took a step backwards. They came upon me like a pack of wilder beasts, funnelling around my bare toes and past me. I was frozen in terror, watching as they took each step by getting into every crevice. Every angle of the carpet. I was dreaming. I had to be still dreaming. I pulled and pinched at the skin of my elbow, tears welling in my eyes as I listened to the disgusting scuttling and willing myself to wake up.
That was when he came into view. That same, pale, ghostly face that I had seen in my dreams a moment ago was lit up like the moon in the night-sky. His eyes were

wide and menacing as he regarded me for a moment before starting to ascend the stairs.
I tried to scream, but it got caught in my throat. Panic bubbled in my chest, and I could feel my heart pulsing with adrenaline as I stumbled over myself trying to get back down the hall. I could hear the crunch of cockroach bodies as I stepped backwards.

"No," I whispered, "No."

I could hear each stair creak with the sound of squelching leather. I was aware that I was getting close to the end of the hallway and my options were limited. I was sweating so much, the thick t-shirt I was wearing was sticking to my back and I could feel my skin itching. I reached for the door handle to the bedroom. Bugs. So many bugs nipping and pulling at me with bloodthirstiness.
He was just making the top of the stairs. I could see the tips of his black boots as he rounded the corner. I couldn't breathe.
Whimpering, I fell into the bedroom and slammed the door shut.
It was too much for me. My head was spinning and I couldn't think straight. I pushed back up against the wall

by the door and my knees gave way, leaving me to slide down the wall into a crouch. My head in my heads, I waited for him to get me. Like it was a game of tag and he was it, this mysterious man who had broken into the house and my dreams.

I was crying now. Sobbing. I could hear every footstep he took, every stomp, as he made his way up the hallway. And then, silence.

My breathing sped up as I prepared to scream. Maybe someone would hear me out here. Maybe.

The door creaked open. My body was wracked with panic, broken with a thick resignation that I was too weak to fight this.

"Polly?"

How did he know my name? I was still sobbing. My throat was beginning to get hoarse.
He shook my shoulder and I rattled against the wall.

"Polly, it's okay."

That was Tom's voice.

I slowly pulled my hands away from my face and looked up at him, he was crouched next to me looking concerned. The light in the hallway had been turned on and brightness flooded the room. Not an insect in sight.
"What?" I sniffed, confused.
"What the fuck is wrong with you? What happened?" He was rubbing at my shoulder softly, his actions not matching his tone.
"Where is he?" I croaked, "The man…he…was on the stairs."
He looked freaked. I felt uneasy at the thought that he was still in the house and Tom wasn't taking me seriously. I could still see the depth of his black irises as they looked up at me from that bottom stair. I shivered.
"What are you on about?" Tom scoffed, "There's no one here."
"Check," I begged, trying to pull myself up, "Check right now."
"There's no one here, Polly," Tom stood up abruptly, "I was downstairs the whole time!"

"No," I shook my head, "No. I saw him. I keep seeing him."

"Seeing who?"

"A man, with a white face. He's done bad things. I can feel it."

Tom sighed, "You've been drinking."

"No," I could feel my face turning red with anger, "I have not. He's taking kids."

"I'm sorry?"

I didn't know where that had come from either. Maybe I had put two and two together and made five, but I had a strong feeling that this man, whatever he was, was connected to Rowan's disappearance. A man breaking into houses in Mountmend, it was all too coincidental. I was aware that I may have been assuming, but the way Mrs Wearne's eyes had shown fear was all too familiar to me.

"You heard me," I stood firm, "You need to call the police."

Tom let out a scoff, "Polly, it's 4am. There is nobody in this house except me and you. I suggest you get back into bed now and try to calm down. Do you want a hot water bottle? Would that help?"

"A hot water bottle? I'm not on my period, Tom!"

"I didn't suggest you were." He sounded frustrated, as he threw back the covers and held his hand out.
I felt defeated. All the fight I had felt dissipated from my body like steam, and I relaxed slightly. At least he was here with me. At least, when this man inevitably returned, he could see for himself. I took Tom's hand and let him guide me into bed.
He tucked me in like I was a toddler, wrapping me up like I was in a tight cocoon. Maybe he was trying to stop me getting out again.
I didn't take my hand off of him the rest of the night. I wanted to make sure he was still there. When he rolled over, I moved my hand to his back. When he turned back the other way, I moved my hand to his shoulder. I didn't want to be left by myself, not considering I was too traumatised to actually sleep anyway.

At 6am, I got myself up and went downstairs. It was light now, so I felt comfortable doing it. Summer was coming and so was my birthday. It was Friday.
I didn't feel like celebrating as I made myself a cup of tea and settled onto the sofa. My eyes felt heavy with lack of sleep and my body was exhausted. My skin still felt puffy where I had been crying so much.

Tom didn't get up until 10, and when he came downstairs, he announced he was going out again.
"Where?" I grumbled. We'd spent more time apart than together since we'd got there.
"The supermarket."
"Why?"
"What is this? A quiz? What's the right answer?"
I winced at his sarcasm. It wasn't playful, it was mean. He had no hint of humour on his face.
"I just don't want to be on my own at the moment."
"It's broad daylight, Pol."
I shrugged, "I guess." I couldn't be bothered to argue anymore. No matter what I said, he would still go. As much as I didn't want to be sat in Conan's house alone, with my thoughts just as much as with the house, I didn't want Tom to think I was any crazier than he'd already made out. I was somewhat embarrassed about the night before.
He put his shoes on, grabbed his keys, waved goodbye and disappeared through the front door without another word between us. A couple of minutes later I heard the engine start and the car revved, wheels taking up the dirt.
 I jumped up from the sofa, opportunity rife in the air. I ran to the kitchen and started picking up boxes full of

paperwork that had been neatly packed away in the "keep" pile. I tipped them onto the kitchen table and spread them about eagerly, looking for something, anything, that would tell me anything about this man that had been in the house. Even about Rowan. I was looking for anything and everything.

There was paper everywhere in a loose cacophony of documents and photos, covering the entirety of the tabletop as I wracked through it, not caring about ripped corners or creases that would inevitably give me away later.

There was nothing of significance there. It was all old details of insurance details and pensions, details about the house and such like. It was fruitless, but I was on a mission.

I left my mess in the kitchen and took the stairs two at a time, blowing the doors open to Conan's bedroom like it was a raid. Things had been moved, were missing. All that was left was just the furniture and a bed, no sign that it was ever lived in. I went straight for the drawers again, where I had found the newspaper clippings. Empty this time. I then moved over to the bedside tables. Inside the top drawer on the right-hand side of the bed was a bible. It was thick and leather bound, with the words "The Holy

Bible" inscribed across the cover in shiny gold lettering. Without thinking too much about it, I opened it to where the book felt thickest, like there was something trapped in the middle.

My breath caught in my throat as I stared down at the man who had tormented my dreams.

It was him. Absolutely and irrevocably. Those same dark eyes, like he was soulless. The turned-up collar of a thick leather jacket, the thought of its noise making me feel sick. It wasn't a photo. It was too old for that. It was an artist's impression, made up of lines and shadows sketched in graphite. This illustration was fraying around the edges, like it had travelled through time and felt the consequences. There was nothing else present. Not even a date or signature on the back.

The way I thought about dreams, warped memories of something you had witnessed or felt during the day that manifests itself in your subconscious. I wracked my brain to see if I had seen this mysterious figure's face before, in the church or the bakery or in a photo frame somewhere. It was nowhere else. He had a distinctive face that made me shudder, and I knew that I would be able to recall it if I had seen it before. This threw my entire theory of dreams out the window and turned it into the terrifying idea that this man had crawled into my subconscious of his own accord.

I needed answers.

I took the drawing and closed the bible with a thud, throwing it back into the drawer where I found it and slamming it shut.
I ran down the stairs towards the front door and pulled my boots on quickly, grabbing my backpack and keys with haste.
I didn't even worry that I'd locked the door, I simply took off down the path with a heavy and frightening burden in my back pocket.

When I got to Lena's, her car was sat in the back driveway. The back gate flew open as I ploughed through it, alerting Lena to my presence as she stood by the sink in front of the kitchen window. She looked at me, eyebrows raised, concerned.
She pulled the door open just as I got there.
"Hey Polly," She said, in her sing song voice, "Is everything okay?"

I moved past her, panting. All the adrenaline quickly drained from my body, and I suddenly felt incredibly stupid.

"Uh," I stuttered, "I came over because, I have some questions."

"Questions?" Lena lent on the kitchen island with her hands clasped together, she didn't look worried at all.

"Yes," I said, "I want you to tell me who this is."

I pulled the picture from my pocket and placed it down on the island, sliding it across to her.

Her face was merely inquisitive as she picked it up and examined it. I was so untrusting. I read her face as best I could for any hint of recognition.

"Uh, yes. I think I do."

"You do?" I was surprised.

"Where did you get this, Polly?" She asked.

"That doesn't matter," I was anxious, hopping from foot to foot, "Listen, I just need to know."

"What's wrong?" She placed the photo back down and came towards me, "You seem upset."

"I'm not. I'm fine. I'm just, tired." I swallowed.

"Let's sit down shall we? Tea?"

I nodded.

I waited for Lena in the lounge whilst she brewed our tea. My leg bounced up and down with impatience. She placed my mug gently on the coffee table when she was done, taking a seat next to me on the sofa. She crossed her legs, holding her tea gently in her lap with both hands.
"Talk to me." She said, gently.
I sighed, "I want to know who that is in that photo."
It was Lena's turn to sigh, "Okay. That's Leucum Pengally."
I swallowed. "I went to see Mrs Wearne, you know? Rowan's mother. She said that Pengally had something to do with her son's disappearance." I had no idea why I was suddenly admitting this. Lena had one of those faces that made you open up. Earnest and forgiving.
Lena scoffed, "Really? She's cookoo as an old clock, Polly. It's just an old wive's tale, all of it."
"Tell me," I pleaded, "The tale."
She sighed, "It is just that, a tale. Mrs Wearne is full of stories and blame."
I waited patiently, and Lena sighed again.
"Okay," She started, sitting forward, "I'll tell you."

"A couple of hundred years ago, there was a Cornish man who used to live in Mountmend called Leucum Pengally.

He was born here to a poor Mother and a Father who died tragically in an accident. He grew up here, not the best childhood by any means. He would often go hungry, his Mother too depressed at his Father's death to make end's meet. His Mother eventually died from tuberculosis when he was 17. He met and married a local girl from the village and was desperate to provide for her. She came from money, you see. It was one of the conditions that he was allowed to marry her. That he would look after her the same way her own Father did. She couldn't see him for what he was then.

He was an innately horrible man with a horrible disposition. He was not much liked amongst the village on account of his greed. As he grew up, he would do whatever he could to cheat the villagers out of money, not caring if they barely had a pot to piss in. He left them starving, took their crops. Any livestock in the fields, he claimed. He distributed food and withheld food depending on his mood. By the time his son was born, he was sitting on a small fortune. He cared for no one like he cared for his son. His successor. He believed that the Pengally name was to fly through generations and generations, all starting with his son. He was the only one in which he showed mercy.

As his son grew up, people despised Leucum Pengally more and more. He would show off his lavish clothes and his fancy house, all with the money he had cheated out of the villagers. He would invite nearby aristocrats for extravagant dinners as the villagers went hungry. They resented him. The local rich families never accepted him. Eventually his wife started to resent him too.
She was a kind lady by nature and decided that she could no longer love a man who was so selfish and heartless. She left him, taking his son with her.
He tried tirelessly to chase them down, but to no avail. The rumour was that she left on a boat off the coast. He went mad with grief and rage, coming down even more harshly on those who dared to wrong him or step in his path. The villagers lived in terror of Leucum Pengally. They had nothing, but he would still take what he could from them.
One night, in a mad rage and drunken stupor, he attempted to kidnap one of the young boys in the village. He was the same age that his young son had been. The village was distraught. Of course, he was caught before he even reached the hilltop. Authorities brought him back, put him in jail. But it didn't last. He had a fortune, and he

paid the courts to let him go free on the basis that he would "repent".
He did go free, but he lived out the remainder of his life in his little mansion, grieving for his missing wife and son. He died there, but not after hiding his fortune so that none of the village could ever reach it. There was no heir to his fortune. People have tried, but no one has been able to locate his missing riches.
Legend has it that he still haunts the village of Mountmend to escape the fires of hell for his sins. He cannot rest, as he wails across the valley for his son. They say you can hear it late at night echoing across the hillsides. It sounds like an animal being tortured."

Her synopsis hung in the air, waiting to be taken in. I sat there, staring at Lena as she sipped on her tea with her eyebrows raised. I was pulled into the mystics of an old tale, passed through centuries of ancestry and changing slightly with every recollection. Like Chinese Whispers.
I was confused, "And, that's the man in the picture?"
"Mhm," Lena nodded, "He's a bit infamous around here."
"Was he real?"

"I don't think so," Lena shrugged, "He doesn't have a grave, or anything to indicate that he actually *lived* here. It's just a story."

I was stumped, quite truly. I expected Leucum Pengally to be a modern man, someone who lived in the village. For him to be involved in Rowan Wearne's disappearance, he needed to be *real*. I felt reassured by Lena's take, and her storytelling, which made me believe that Mrs Wearne might be more nuts than I had originally given her credit for.

"Where did you get it, the photo?"

I fell back into the room from my musings.

"Nowhere. I just found it when we were shredding things that's all."

Lena didn't look surprised, as she placed her tea gently down onto the coffee table.

She hesitated for a moment before changing the subject completely, "What do you want for your birthday?"

8

When you're overtired, two glasses of wine feel eerily like five, and after dinner that night I felt more at ease that a strange man, Leucum Pengally, was *not* going to break into the house considering he'd been dead hundreds of years. That's if he even existed at all. He floated through my dreams like a weird premonition that was an echo of something I'd seen somewhere. A face in a newspaper…or a drawing hidden within the pages of a bible.
I was certainly tired, and the wine was making it worse. I could hear Tom moving about upstairs, and I had every intention of making it up the stairs and into the bedroom, but as soon as I relaxed into the sofa, I found myself

sliding down until my head was rested on the arm rest and I was drifted off to sleep.

I dreamt erratically.
I was wandering through a tall forest, filled with fir trees that created a green canopy, cutting the stars from my view. The floor crunched under my footsteps. It was so quiet, and the air was thick with solitude, every step I took echoed between the tree trunks. I didn't recognise where I walked, it was all unfamiliar. There was a light mist that seemed to rise from the floor like I'd tripped a gas switch.
I was stuck in a trance-like state, just swaying through the trees like I was drunk. My foot hit an uplifted root and I found myself falling, almost in slow motion. I hit the ground with a little yelp. Everything went black.
When I opened my eyes again. I was on my back, looking up at that same blanket of tree branches above me. I was still in the woods.
I felt achy and out of sorts. I tried to move, but I felt stuck. My arms and legs were spread out like I was a starfish, pulled to their maximum length in a big stretch. I couldn't seem to move my arms and legs inwards towards me. I

could hear the leaves crackle and crunch underneath my body as I wriggled.
I turned my head slowly to the right and tried to lift my hands off the ground, but they were stuck. I realised that my wrist was bound by a thick vine. In a panic, I flicked my head to the left and found the other hand in the same binds. Panic coursed through me like a spreading fire, piercing my heart with adrenaline until it was pounding in my chest and ears. I urgently tugged at the restraints, whimpering. I could feel the branches cutting my skin as I thrashed against my bonds.

 I felt a presence moving next to me, as real as the skin on my bones. I could hear his deep breathing and that familiar sound of leather crunching together. I didn't need to see him to know who it was who'd put me here. Who would soon be standing over me. I was laying there trembling and vulnerable. I felt exposed.
His face appeared over mine, ominously appearing into view slowly. Acid pooled in my stomach and I had that familiar salivation feeling like I was going to throw up. I gulped it back. My mouth continued to sweat.
"What do you want?" I gasped, "What do you want?"

He said nothing, and just stared into my eyes. His face was crusty, marked with a thousand blemishes. That familiar scar looking even more disgusting up close. I could see not a hint of soul behind his eyes. No emotion. His irises were black as the night sky. My fighting was fruitless when he so clearly had no cause for human empathy. He stood there, leering over me as I lay helplessly strapped to the ground. The air felt humid and thick with heat. I struggled to take a breath. My lungs burned. He did nothing. Just looked down upon me like I was a piece of meat he was getting ready to chop up and devour.

"Please." I begged. I was sweating, or were they tears? Suddenly, darkness enveloped me like I was being pulled under water by a strong current. I was sucked further and further downwards towards the centre of the earth. Blackness fraying the edges of my vision. I was screaming, but nothing was coming out.

With a whoosh, I was catapulted into myself, and I shot upright, abruptly awake with no recollection of where I actually was. I was dripping in a thick sweat that made my hair stick to the back of my neck like a slimy glue. I couldn't catch my breath. The house was dark and creaking, I was on the sofa. I scrambled across the sofa to reach for the lamp, not caring what clattered to the floor in

the process. I flicked the lamp on and looked around the room hastily. There was no one there. I fumbled about the sofa looking for my phone. I clicked it to life. 6am.
I got up and pulled back the curtains to the living room, letting the light flood in enough to ease my nerves. I stood there for a moment, staring out at the forest on the horizon. Breathing in. Breathing out. I felt sick.

My head was still spinning. Maybe it was the house, or the village, that was bringing Leucum Pengally into my dreams. It was sending me spiralling. But I couldn't go. Or could I go? I clutched at my stomach. Every encounter with him felt *real*. I was a lawyer. Any rationality I had in my head was slowly dissipating with every thought, every dream. Maybe that's why I was still where I was, an apprentice, 5 years later. Night terrors. That's all this was. Was I trying to rationalise?
Before I could wallow even deeper in my misgivings, I heard a floorboard creak. I whipped round with bated breath.
"Polly?"
Tom appeared in the doorway. I let out a long breath.
"What the fuck is wrong with you? You look terrible. Have you even slept?"

I swallowed, "Yes. But Tom, I had the worst nightmare. I keep having them actually."
"Okay."
"There's this man," I started, "I have his photograph."
"What?" He looked dumbfounded.
"A drawing. I found it upstairs in the…"
"You went through my Grandfather's things?" Tom raised an eyebrow.
I was trying to get my story straight, but my head was still swarming with a million thoughts at once that I was struggling to put them into any ascertainable order.
"Yes, but it was only in the draw. In the bible."
"You're not making any sense."
"The drawing was in the bible. It was a man. It's a man named Leucum Pengally. Mrs Wearne said that he was involved in Rowan's disappearance so I went to talk to Lena about it. Now I keep seeing him when I go to sleep."
"What is wrong with you, Polly?" Tom looked angry, "You are making no sense. What you are talking about is a myth. A tale that has been told round here for decades. It has absolutely no substance to it whatsoever."
"I know, but…"
"Mrs Wearne is a crazy lady. She went crazy when she lost Rowan and she continues to get worse every day."

"That's what Lena said, but…"

"You're getting yourself wound up over nothing. He's not real, Polly."

"Will you let me finish?" I snapped.

"No," Tom turned around and made his way towards the kitchen, "No, I'm not going to. This stops now."

I followed him. The air was thick with an angry tension, and I could feel it bubbling in my chest and threatening to rise like bile. Frustration encircled both of us.

"What the *fuck*! I'm not a child, Tom!"

"You might as well be," he span round, his finger jabbing towards me, "I can't leave you alone for 5 minutes before you're rummaging through my dead grandad's things!"

"That's not what this is about! I only went in there because I was worried for our safety. *My* safety."

"Safety from what, Polly? Some weird man who lived here hundreds of years ago? You are seriously losing it."

He started to rummage through dishes in the sink, they clattered around and made me wince with each crash. He flicked the tap on angrily. He always did this, acted like he didn't care. Carried on with his everyday life after saying something hurtful. He knew how to switch off. He could go to bed angry. He could shove it all in a little box in the back of his mind and not touch it ever again.

I gulped, "I'm not crazy."
He didn't respond.
"If you don't believe me, then I'll go down to Lena's."
"No," Tom's focus was back on me immediately, "No. You are not to burden my sister with all this anymore than you already have. You are not leaving this house today."
"You can't just lock me up here like I'm in prison!" I wailed.
"You need to rest. Look at you." His tone altered; it was softer, more concerned. His expression loosened and for a moment I did believe he was genuinely concerned.
"I'm fine." I contested.
"You need to sleep, upstairs in a proper bed. Have a shower and sleep for a few hours." He caressed the top of my arms, shaking me gently.
I melted into his touch. "Okay." I squeaked.
I had no energy to fight him anymore. Every time we disagreed, or fought, it felt like we got nowhere. He didn't listen to me. My energy could only go so far before I didn't understand the point anymore, and I'd rather have him on my side than not. He was a comforting element that I couldn't let go of. It was easier to relent when I knew that he never would.

"Okay," Tom began to guide me towards the stairs, "Go and settle. I'll bring you a cup of tea."
I did shower. But I wasn't showering thinking about how I was going to go to sleep, I was thinking about how I could get out of here. I needed to clear my head.

Tom came up with a cup of tea, but to his dismay I had changed into a pair of jeans and a hoodie rather than pyjamas.
"Thanks." I said, taking the cup of tea from him carefully.
"Don't fancy sleeping?"
"No," I said, "I'm going for a walk. I need some air."
"Is that wise?"
I nodded. I sipped the tea, but it was still too hot for me.
"Suit yourself. But, don't go too far out." Tom looked worried. I indulged in that.
"I won't," I assured, "I'll come back soon, I'm just going to walk."
I could feel Tom's eyes on me from the living room window as I was rounding the corner down the drive and out of sight. Once I was sure that I'd cleared the tree line, I picked up the pace.

I was not bothered at what Tom had said about Lena. She had given me straight answers before, reassured me, and after the dream that I had I needed someone to at least listen to me.
My phone rang.
I answered, "Hi, Mum."
"Where are you?" She asked, "You seem out of breath."
"Just out for a walk."
"Okay. Listen, I've been thinking, maybe you should come back home now."
"What makes you say that?"
"Tomorrow is the first birthday where I won't see you, and I just feel like you should be here with me." She sounded pained.
I sighed. There were so many questions I had, and a couple of days left to think about them. As much as I yearned for my Mother, I also yearned for Tom, no matter how difficult he was being. It was my birthday, and I wanted to spend it by his side too. I couldn't blame him; he'd had a tough week. I was like a kicked puppy, still following its owner around with reckless infatuation. How foolish of me.

"I can't just yet, Mum. I can't leave Tom and Lena. I'll be back next week once they have put the house on the market."

"Okay, darling," she sounded deflated, "But please pop round here as soon as you get back."

"I will, Mum."

She sighed in relief, "I'll call you tomorrow, but Happy Birthday Polly."

"Thank you. I love you."

"I love you too."

I ended the call.

I missed my Mum so much, because I was sure that she would listen to what I was going through without judgement. Her fantastical imagination would allow her to see more possibilities and offer me some kind of plan, like she always has done. She would say to me that there was always a solution, like a novel that starts with an introduction, a problem, and then a resolution. In most cases. She would say that I would have to get through the problem to reach the resolution, and that if nothing happened in the novel it wouldn't be very good. That's how I viewed my problems a lot of the time, as pages in a story.

I marched myself into the village and across the green. For a Saturday, it was pretty quiet. A few people milled around outside the post office, and another left the bakery with a bag full to the brim. I didn't pay attention to the eyes I could feel on my back, following me as I reached the edge of the village and down the road towards Lena's house. It was warmer now, as Spring turned into Summer as it did every year around my birthday. The Summer Solstice, a spectacle observed in so many cultures. The air was humidifying with every moment that went by.

I pulled my hoodie off and tied it around my waist. Lena's house came into view.

I instinctively head to the back gate. I could see Lena's head bobbing as she got out of her car, slamming the door shut. She fumbled with her keys and a bag of shopping. She jumped when she saw me.

"You scared me!" She frowned, hand to her chest in feigned dramatic shock.

"Sorry."

"What are you doing here?" Her expression morphed into her familiar one of concern, "Are you okay?"

I hesitated.

"Come in," Lena gestured towards the back gate, "You look tired."

I followed behind her like a duckling, following its mother with blind faith. My shoulders were heavy with sleep and the burden of deep thought. I must have looked a wreck. The first thing that she did was put the kettle on, before putting her shopping away neatly into its designated spots in the cupboards. It looked like something off Pinterest, glass jars with cork lids and labelled spices. Even that was too much for me to bare. Too neat. Too much.

I didn't say anything. I watched her go about her normal life. Her life free from the existential dread that I felt in mine. The lack of sleep was itching parts of my brain that I didn't want scratched.

"Tell me." She looked over earnestly.

I sighed, "I saw him again. I keep seeing him. Everywhere."

"Who?"

"Leucum Pengally. From the picture."

Lena pursed her lips in thought. "Okay," she reasoned, "let's think about this. It was a scary story, maybe you were more afraid of it than you thought? Now you can name him it feels more real?"

"Maybe. I don't feel like it's a dream. It feels real. It feels as real as you or I."

"Were you asleep when you were experiencing this? Then it was a dream."

I growled in frustration, "I can't take it anymore, Lena."

"Polly…"

"No." I hopped to my feet. My head felt swollen, like it was getting bigger and bigger, about to pop. I gripped at my temples with my fingertips.

"Calm down, Polly. Take a breath."

"I'm not crazy!" I certainly felt it.

"I know you're not." Lena was on her feet now, her hands on my shoulders. Her face was inches from mine. There was not a smudge nor mark across her skin, like a smooth oil painting it glowed.

I sniffed, "I'm sorry."

Something in her expression changed. Hardened. It scared me. A pit opened up in my stomach as she looked into my eyes.

"Leave." She said.

"What?"

"Go." This was a different Lena. The softness to her tone had dissipated, left behind a monotony that I was unfamiliar with hearing from her. It was like time had paused.

I was clueless. I studied her face, she was serious.

"Go? Where?"
"You should leave, Polly," She stepped back, running a hand through her hair, "You should go home now. It's too much for you here."
I hesitated.
"Grandad's death, the funeral," She paused, "Leucum Pengally. Trauma can do funny things to someone. Just, please, think about going."
My throat was dry, "Okay."
She seemed relieved, "Okay. I know it's your birthday tomorrow. Have you got anything planned?" The switch in topic made my head spin.

I hadn't. I thanked Lena for her comfort when I heard Arthur's car pull onto the drive with the scraping of tires on gravel. I slipped out the front door. Lena said it was probably best given how upset I'd been. I didn't want to speak to Arthur anyway.

Speaking with Lena had not had the desired effect that I had hoped, and I was still a flurry. The way that Lena had told me to go, there was something in her eyes that sent me into a panic that started in the tips of my toes and travelled through to the top of my head. Every horn, every car door or dog barking, made me jolt and shudder. I felt myself start to dissociate. The world around me felt like a dream, fuzzy around the edges. I focused all my energy on getting back to Conan's house. One foot in front of the other. I wanted to speak to Tom. I wanted to pack my bags and get into the car. Adrenaline coursed through my veins with a savage vengeance, keeping me in line even though I wanted to sprint. I forced myself to walk normally across the village and up the dirt lanes. Cars passed, but I didn't dare look at their drivers or their passengers. My teeth chattered together making my jaw ache. I wasn't too far away as the dirt turned to gritty gravel.

As I reached the house and bounded up the steps, the door was already wide open. Tom was pulling at the collar on his jacket.

I swallowed, "Are you going somewhere?"

He sighed, "Yes. I'm going down to Lena's."

"I've just been there."

He didn't respond.

"Can you hold on a minute? I really need to talk to you." I stepped inside.

He placed a tentative hand on my arm, "We'll talk later, okay? I said I'd help Arthur and I'm already late."

I was buzzing with anxious energy, and I could feel myself tensing with every breath I took.

"Please?" I tried.

"I really need to go, Pol," He kissed my cheek, "It'll be okay."

I wanted to stop him. As he pulled away from me and shut the door behind him. I stood stock still in the hallway, my hands balled into fists at my sides. I let him go, *again*. I should have put my foot down this time. I should have said no. I felt the knots of frustration forming in my shoulders. I paced it to the living room and peered through the window. It was 6pm and the sky was turning a plush pink, the sun hovering on the horizon over the distant hillside. I watched Tom walk away with his hands in his pockets and his shoulders hunched. To my surprise, he didn't turn right down the tree-lined pathway. Instead, he headed across the green towards the opening of the woods.

I didn't stop for thought. I let him head downwards, and into the opening of the woodland. He disappeared into the frow. I staggered to the front door and flung it open. My heart thumped in my chest with a frightening pound that I could hear in my ears. Even as I crept across the dirt towards the grass, I found myself crouching in case Tom had decided to turn back. I hadn't decided exactly what I would do if that happened, but the urgency of the

situation outweighed the furiousness he would feel at me following him. More fuel for him to call me crazy.
When I reached the edge of the woodland, I took one look back up at the house. It sat atop the hill like a castle. Unguarded, yet an ominous presence that made me feel concerned. Even with this foreboding feeling, it still felt like a sanctuary compared with the woods that I hadn't yet explored.
As I pushed on, I couldn't see Tom anymore. I was following blind through crunching twigs and dust. Dodging rogue branches and trunks. I was breathing heavily and remembering the dream, the surroundings bringing me to the brink of panic. I begged myself to stay in control, follow the sound of crunching and echoing footsteps. The trees overhung with the weight of their leaves, like thin skeletal arms intertwining above me in decoration.
I was working on pure adrenaline. Stumbling around like I was on something sinister. It was getting darker with every moment, that dusky grey that hangs in the air and before you know it you can't make out your hand in front of your face.
As I walked, I could hear more noise. The sound of chattering. A distant glow ahead of me that flickered

through the tree trunks. I quickly realised that it was fire. It quivered against the blackness starting to envelope the forest and faintly lit the way forwards like a beacon.

I stopped dead in my tracks, as the voices were louder now. I could make out shadows, figures through the trees. Ahead, there was a clearing. Full of people. People moved about slowly, like a strange shadow dance. Some were sitting on what appeared to be lumpy rocks, others milled together in clusters. I squinted into the smoke-filled dusk. My curiosity hummed under the surface of my skin, dragging my feet forward with an urge that seemed to cancel out every rational thought. I stopped at the treeline to the clearing, my body tucked behind the trunk whilst I peered around it as best I could. I hoped the darkness would be a good camouflage.

My throat tightened as my eyes began to make out faces. Every person was shrouded in a black, floor length cloak. Hoods draped down their backs, covered in a thick gold embroidery. It was mesmerising. I swallowed hard, my eyes taking in the features of the baker who'd made my sausage rolls. The woman who had interrupted our business transaction was cleaning her steamed up glasses on her cloak sleeve. I remembered Mr Horne who Lena had pointed out to me on the first day, and the man with the walking stick that was propped up precariously against his leg as he sat on a rock. I flickered between bodies, familiar faces from Conan's funeral and eventually, Clement Ward.

Clement Ward was standing tall, the only man amongst this congregation to be wearing a thick crown of vines. I was catapulted into a memory, a memory of gazing at the same ring of vines I'd seen on every fireplace in the village. Bile bubbled in my stomach.

He was shaking hands with his peers, a thin smile dancing on his lips. Almost a smirk.

From the back end of the clearing, two figures glided across the ground as if they were floating. They were the only two with their hoods firmly atop their heads. As they reached the orange glow of the crackling fire their faces became more apparent. I blinked harshly, resisting the urge to rub my eyes. My breath caught as I saw the familiar expressions of the twins. Tom and Lena. I was blindsided. I couldn't accept what I was seeing, squeezing my eyes shut and letting them open again until I was seeing stars. I couldn't work out which feeling to feel first, the feeling of utter betrayal that Tom had been keeping something so intense from me or the feeling of being absolutely stumped at what I was witnessing. I had been at Lena's house not a few hours ago, drinking tea whilst she comforted me. I was so utterly confused. The late night disappearances and the early morning returns. Tom was more of a liar than I ever thought he could be.

Clement greeted them both by shaking their hands firmly. He patted Tom on the shoulder like a father might do to his son. Tom's expression was one of pride. He stood a little bit taller than he usually did, his shoulders nice and his neck long.

Clement stood in front of the twins and turned to his flock with a flourish, arms outstretched, voice booming:

"Hush now. Hush. Ladies and Gentlemen, the Solstice is almost upon us."

People muttered amongst themselves.

"The time is almost near."

"But will it work?" It was Lena's voice. She stepped forward with a concerned look upon her face.

"Will he accept it?" This was another voice amongst the congregation, a woman's voice, "Pengally. Will he accept the sacrifice?"

My mind whirled. S*acrifice?* Is this what they do? Put a lamb on a slab and slice its neck? I tried to swallow, but my mouth was so incredibly dry. I attempted to lick my lips instead just to bring back some moisture.
Clement Ward cleared his throat, "I can assure you, that this is the only way. Cows, pigs, sheep, it is not enough. He is coming, and he is taking your children. Do you wish that for your neighbours? Your family and friends?"
The congregation was silent. Some looked to floor, twiddling their thumbs. Mrs Wearne had warned of this, that Leucum Pengally took Rowan. This was madness. Words left my lips in a whisper, *"What The Fuck."*
Clement whisked round to face Tom, who stood with his hands clasped in front of him. Furiousness clouded my vision as I studied his face. Emotionless now, as per usual.
"Is she ready?" Clement asked.
Tom nodded, "Yes."
She. My throat was closing off, I was puffing into the air trying to catch a breath. I wasn't stupid, it didn't take me long to put two and two together. It was me. They were talking about me. Here they were, the only person in the village not present in their gathering was me. I was shaking my head slowly. I started to feel dizzy.

Clement pulled a blade from under his cloak, lifting it into the air like it was the sword of Excalibur. The gold handle was matted as Clement gripped it tightly with whitened knuckles. The shiny, silver blade glinted in the roar of the flames as he lowered it over the fire, speaking in a tongue I didn't understand.

Obsecro, benedicat hoc ferrum.

The onlookers erupted into a low hum, eyes closed in concentration.
Although I was bewitched by the strangeness of what I was witnessing, I knew I had to go. That blade was calling me, its voice echoing across the forest and pulling me in by my heart. I started to shuffle backwards, my back scratching against the trees as I failed to take my eyes off what was happening. I began to speed up.

As I was backing away, the flicker of the flames fading from my vision, I was swallowed by darkness. I froze as I was suddenly senseless. I couldn't see, it was all just outline. All I could hear was my own raspy breath.

As if in a nightmare, a hellish wail echoed across the woods. It was a screech, a painful howl that could be mistaken for a ravenous animal after its prey. It shook through me and pricked at my skin. I shivered from the tip of my head through to my toes.

I took off. Fleeing like a wanted prisoner through the trees. I imagined being chased by an animal, jumping from tree root to stump and snarling as it stalked me through the undergrowth. I couldn't see where I was going, the only direction was downwards towards the bottom of the hillside. I reasoned with myself, if I just kept running in the same direction, I would get to Conan's.

I did fall a few times, ripping the knees on my jeans with the adrenaline covering up any pain from grazes. I could see the opening of the treeline illuminated by the moonlight. It was a homestretch, my pace not faltering as I leapt out of the forest and scrambled up the hillside. As I ran, Conan's house came into view. I started to cry with relief. A light was on in the hallway from where I had left in a hurry, illuminating the way like a beacon of hope. Like a lighthouse guiding a lost ship through the maze of rocks. I made my way across the gravel pathway and

through the front door with a burst, the door smacking the wall as it flung wide open. I forced myself to take deep breaths.
"Ok," I said to myself, "Bag. I need my bag."
I took the stairs two at a time, pulling my duffel out from under the bed and flinging it onto the duvet. I started shoving things in roughly. I wasn't concerned about what I was missing, and after a minute or two I realised how ludicrous it was that I was even packing in the first place. I zipped it up quickly and ran down the stairs grabbing the keys to the car from the kitchen table and heading for the door.
The car clicked as it unlocked, and I threw the bag into the back. There wasn't a lot going through my mind, I was entirely focused on the task in front of me. It was the quietest my mind had been since we arrived in Mountmend. Maybe even months prior. My hands shook as I closed the passenger door, and I ran a hand through my hair in an attempt to calm myself down.
I jogged round the back of the car and pulled open the driver's door, but just as I was about to throw a look over my shoulder, I felt the roughness of arms around my waist. I lurched backwards with a yelp. Fright surged through me

like electricity, making my legs thrash. I twisted my neck as much as I could, the arms that
constricted me belonged to the one person that I hoped that it wasn't.
It was Tom.
His stoic expression made me shiver, my spine arching as he continued to drag me back across the gravel.

"Stop," I tried to scream again, "Please, Tom, please."

He clamped a hand over my mouth. Hands that had once been so gentle with me, so loving. He hadn't held me with roughness, always with tenderness. My brain was jumping through memories of us curled up together, legs intertwined as we snoozed before our alarms woke us up for the day. The early stages, the honeymoon period of our time together. It was too much for me to bare. An ultimate betrayal that almost made me give up the fight, almost.
"Help me with her, then!" He barked.
Two men emerged from the darkness and took one of my legs each, I tried to kick gravel at them, but they caught my thrashing legs before I could do anything further. They restrained me like I wasn't the first person they had ever

restrained. I was being carried back into Conan's house with little to no care, my hips bruised on the door frame. I breathed heavily into Tom's hand. I started to feel lightheaded as my nose took the brunt of every breath. It is hard to articulate the feeling of utter dread that comes from being restrained, lashing your limbs but the only thing being achieved is your energy slowly dissipating and the thought of capitulating and becoming a rag doll in the arms of my captors.

I thought of my Mother. All alone in that house with only the memories of me to keep her going. Crying whenever she heard certain songs on the radio or dabbing at her eyes gently as she passed the picture of me before prom in the hallway. How devastated she would be. She would be alone. It helped me draw enough breath I needed to keep myself awake.

They took me up the stairs to Conan's bedroom, throwing me onto the bed with a recklessness that you might give to a pillow or a bag, something unbreakable. I felt freer and I attempted to wiggle from grasp, but Tom realised what I was doing and proceeded to kneel on my arms. I screeched as he whipped a hand from my mouth and pulled a dirty rag from his pocket, stuffing it into my mouth with such force I thought I was going to throw up. It tasted like sawdust, I still remember the coarse texture on my tongue.

Tom growled with impatience. I could just about crane my neck enough to see the other two men fumbling about with something. They were hunched over, like they were handling something extremely delicate. I forced myself to breathe deeply through my nose, in for 4 and out for 4.

"Get on with it!" He seethed. The moonlight hit his face and I could see every wrinkle, every spot. This expression, one I had seen so many times when we'd been fighting, was now one I was even more afraid of than ever before. It was cold, unfeeling.

Suddenly, I felt a sharp stab of pain ricochet through my thigh muscle. I groaned, thinking that this was it, that they'd stabbed me and it was all over. I would bleed out on Conan's bed, next to the one person who should have been sheltering me from all of this. There was no one that loved me around this bed, like everyone hopes for.

A warm feeling began to disperse, starting from the wound site and making its way up through every vein. It spread like hot honey through to my fingertips and up to the tops of my ears, making them feel warm and fuzzy. The men pulled back, in the air a syringe with a wet needle. This turned into 2 needles, then 3, then 4. My eyes lost focus. It made my eye sockets ache to keep them open, but there was a desperation I felt in the centre of my chest to try and keep myself awake for as long as possible. A blurry face appeared over mine, features familiar yet untrustworthy. He frowned, taking my chin in his hands and turning my face from left to right.

"Not long now." He muttered.

I felt like a patient on an operating table, suddenly realising that I have no idea what surgery is about to take place. It was too late to go back, for the anaesthetic had taken hold. I was an experiment. A trial. I couldn't hold it back. It washed over me like I was being coddled by sleep's warm and inviting arms. It felt good to lay my head down and let it caress me. It was my Mum's arms.

My eyelids fluttered shut.

"She's out. Let's go."

9

There is an irony in the fact that the best sleep I had the whole time I was in Mountmend was this one. A drug induced, deep sleep that was entirely by force. Maybe that's why I was so willing to embrace it, I let it consume me too fast. I wanted to rest. I was questioning my own sanity so much that my brain needed a break. Its why sleep deprivation is a popular torture method, because after a while you begin to question what's real and what's not. Everything feels like a dream when you are being held from dreaming. Every scenario becomes fuzzy round the edges.

To this day, I'm still not sure if I was dreaming or not. Every few minutes I would see a flicker of light behind my eyelids. I could hear the mumbling of voices as if they were kilometres away and I'd have to strain to hear them, paying attention to their cadences and tones. I was floating. My body felt lighter than air, like I was being carried on a cloud across the night sky. I was quite blissful being in this state of ignorance. "Just 5 more minutes." I would think, allowing myself to be ferried wherever it was that they were taking me. Maybe I was dead. Maybe this was what it was, delightfully floating on the breeze. I was a soul, dust, being carried away. I didn't used to buy into all that so much. My Mum did, believing that there was a higher plane that we travelled to when we snuffed it, maybe this was it.

When I did come to, I really didn't want to. It felt forced. My eyelids were heavy as I heaved them open, squinting above me at what appeared to be a distorted night sky. It slowly came into focus, like I was adjusting a lens. The sour stench of smoke hit my nostrils, heat pummelling the side of my face. My head felt heavy, but even without the ability to move it I was painfully aware that a fire sizzled beside me. My head was swimming. My mouth was dry like sandpaper, and I swallowed twice trying to wet it. Where I was laying felt hard and cold, something was scratching into my back. It wasn't the ground. It didn't feel like the ground. I tried my best to wriggle, but just as in my dream a night or so before, I was bound outstretched by my hands and feet. Panic climbed its way up to my eyes, making them pool over. I started to sob as I thrashed at my ties, trying to break free but instead just causing rope burns that seared my skin.

A cloaked figure appeared into my eyeline. His hood cast his face in shadow.

"What the fuck is going on?" I choaked, I could barely speak.

The figure slowly removed his hood, revealing Tom underneath.

"Tom!" I cry, "Tell me what the fuck is happening!"

He didn't smile, there was no tell. He spoke with a harshness, like he was a teacher telling off a student.

"Crying isn't going to help you."

I swallowed, "Let me out."

"I can't do that, Polly."

"Why? What the *fuck*?"

He came closer to me, looking down at me along his nose like I was a parasite to be eliminated.

"You're here because you need to be. Without you, we'll all die."

"What are you on about? What has any of this got to do with *me*?"

"Leucum Pengally is real, Polly. He is real. He possesses us, possesses our village. He has done now for over 100 years. He kills our crops, he takes our money, and he takes our children."

My eyes were wide, "He can't be."

"Well, he is." Tom growled, "Every year, he demands a sacrifice from us to leave us alone. Pigs, goats, sheep, we even sacrificed a cow. Every year, he would leave us be. One year, my grandfather decided that enough was enough and that we wouldn't live in fear of him anymore. That was the year that Rowan Wearne went missing. He was taken, by Pengally. My Grandfather took the burden on himself, that it was his fault. I'm sure that this had a hand in his heart attack, he felt too guilty to go on."

The air fizzed with anticipation. I couldn't believe what I was hearing.

"We come here," Tom gesticulated to his surroundings, "Every Sunday, to pay homage to him."

"The Church of Pengally was established in 1820, 2 years after Pengally's death." Another voice had taken over, into view came Clement adorned with his crown of thorns. His face was a flushed red.

"Passed through generations, he is celebrated as the protector of Mountmend. We keep him happy, he keeps us healthy, well fed and fruitful."

"This is some kind of cult!" I spat, "You're worshipping a demon of hell!"

"Quiet!" Clement barked, "We do not want to anger him on this night."

"Just as some fear God," Tom continued, "We fear Pengally."

What I was hearing was, of course, ludicrous to anyone who would hear it. I was flashed with memories of Pengally's cold face at the bottom of the stairs in Conan's house, how real it had seemed. I considered a truth in what they were saying, except I believed that this village had taken a curse and turned it into a religion.

"This is where you come in, sweet girl," Clement stepped forward, his fingertips tentatively brushed my cheek and I shivered, "You are tonight's sacrifice."

"Why me? Why would Pengally want me?"

"It has become obvious to the congregation that Pengally is not satisfied with livestock. Think of poor Rowan Wearne, he wants a living soul. Born on the eve of the Summer Solstice, you are the chosen one."

I could have sworn I saw a glimmer in the eyes of Clement Ward as he envisioned carrying out his cruel need to murder and masking it as a common good. This man was unhinged, being blindly followed by people who feared for their own lives. How long would it be before they were on the slab, bound and ready to be killed in the name of evil? I pulled at my ties again.
"Please," I begged, "Let me go. You don't need me."
"Oh, but we do," Clement stepped back, "It is one for the sake of a whole livelihood, it must be done to protect our village and its families."

I whimpered, "Please."

Clement clicked his fingers. There was a flurry, and the same two men who had injected me earlier flittered about before me. In one of their hands was a gold chalice, with golden vines around the rim. They were mixing something, stirring something until they were satisfied. Clement had removed the knife from his cloak, muttering under his breath. I flicked my head from left to right, looking for Tom. Maybe I could appeal to him one last time, maybe deep down he had loved me, and I could reach into that side of him. He was nowhere, disappearing in with the other cloaked figures.

A hand held my mouth open. I tried to bite down, but the grip was strong enough that my jaw ached after just a few moments. The chalice was lifted to my lips and a warm liquid poured into my mouth. It tasted earthy, like a mixture of soil and crispy leaves. It was disgusting, and I almost chucked it back up again. Swallowing it was the last thing I wanted to do, but my choices were limited.

The men moved away from me, like they were performing a strange dance. Clement Ward was left in my eyeline. The knife held aloft above his head. He spoke a strange language I was unfamiliar with, the congregation joining together in a low hum that buzzed in my ears.

The edges of my vision went fuzzy once more, erupting into double. Two Clements stood in front of me. There were two moons in the sky. I blinked fiercely. The familiar sensation of aching eyeballs making me feel uneasy and nauseous.

He was there. Moving towards me like he was a hologram, flickering in and out of existence. I would blink and he would be inches closer. His familiar leather coat hung to his calves. His round, white face like the moon encased with two black crevices for eyes. In a way, I wish that you could have seen him, in this moment. It was like a true demon walked the earth, floating across the ground in a haze of smoke. We've all dreamt of something chasing us, following us through a dark house or abandoned building. We try to run, but it is like trying to run through water. Our legs are heavy, weighted. We try to get away, and we escape before they can get us by waking up. This time, I had no way to get away. I wasn't dreaming, even the haze that had formed in my vision couldn't convince me of that.

I did think I was dreaming when I heard the gunshots. Two, piercing the air like an arrow. I jolted, scrunching my eyes shut. Again, the thought crossed my mind that they had hit me, and I was now dead. That was the sacrifice and Clement had grown impatient. Squeals and screams erupted into the air. The sounds of footsteps indicating chaos. I looked about me, the blurry entrails of people running creating a cacophony of noise. In that moment, I had no idea what was happening, and I just wanted it all to be over. My head was bewildered, and I thought maybe if I shut my eyes and went to sleep, I would wake up somewhere else. Like when my Mum used to carry me asleep from the car as a child, and I woke up all tucked up and cosy in bed.

Just as I was letting myself drift as I had before, a voice pierced the hazy sanctuary I had built in my head.

"Polly."

It didn't matter to me, I was too fleeting. I was dreaming now.

"Polly, please wake up."

Frustrated, I prized my eyes open with all my might. The face hovering over mine was Lena's.
I tried to speak, but the horrible liquid had scratched and burnt my throat.

"It's alright, you're fine, but we need to get you out of here, okay?"

I was confused. My heart wanted to trust her, but my head was painting images of her amongst the congregation wearing a hooded cloak and standing shoulder to shoulder with Tom. I was too exhausted to care. I let her slice the ties, pulling my hands free and lifting me off the wood in which I was led.

The sound of crackling fire and cries seemed to fade as I was draped across her back, one arm across her shoulders and she held my waist. Everything was fizzling out, my muscles relaxing into her as she guided me through the trees.

10

I wish I could tell you how I ended up on the side of the road in a heap just outside Bodmin. I wish I could tell you which route we took, or what Lena said to me on the way. I wish I could tell you if it was even Lena who left me there. A family found me, passing in their campervan on the way back from their family holiday. I was curled up in a ball next to a hedge in nothing but a t shirt and ripped jeans. They said that I was unresponsive, muttering about a man in a leather jacket. I think that, to prevent me scaring their children any more than was necessary, they dropped me outside Bodmin Community Hospital with a bottle of water and an old fleece that they kept in their camper in case of emergencies.

The hospital cleaned me up, and after I'd told them vaguely what had happened, they called the Police. Probably not a surprise, but no one believed what I was saying to them. They couldn't find any traces of a sedative in my system, nothing to suggest that I had been drugged. I even saw one of the policemen that interviewed me scribble, "possible mental health issues" in his notepad. Despite increasing frustration, I did tell myself that they would believe me eventually. All they would need to do is to bring in Tom and they would be able to get his confession. I had no doubts that I would eventually win them over.

I was held at the police station in a small waiting room with bright blue armchairs and a small television on the wall that was showing Sky News. A small, innocent looking receptionist came over periodically to ask if I wanted a drink, tea or coffee. I refused every time, yet she still asked. I didn't think that my stomach had fully recovered.

After a couple of hours of waiting, the same police officer who had been making assumptions on my mental health came to fetch me. He was burly, with a moustache, yet he had a fragility about him that made me feel like I could trust him.
They gestured for me to sit down across from him. Another officer was already waiting, a cup of coffee sitting toasty in his fist. I looked to my left, looking for the one-way glass. There it was, sitting grey and ominous and shooting my reflection back at me. I looked awful, bedraggled. I didn't recognise myself.
"Okay, Polly," The moustached Police Officer started, "We've been in touch with Tom."
I gulped, "Okay."
The Police Officer's exchanged a look. He took a deep breath before speaking, "And he says that you had a bit of trouble down at his grandfather's, is that right?" His Cornish accent was thick and I had to lean forward slightly to process what he was saying.
I paused, "I've told you what happened. A bit of trouble is putting it lightly."
"You see," He leant forward, clasping his hands together, "Tom has said that you suffered a bit of a...mental

breakdown. He said you lost it when he tried to break off your engagement. Ran away, accusing him of all sorts."
My entire body turned cold. I was frowning at these two men, my head cocked to the side in absolute disbelief. I knew that Tom may have not told the truth, but I thought they would have at least brought him in for an interview instead of believing his words without any second thought.
I swallowed, "That never happened. I told you what happened."
I sat firm, squaring my shoulders and making eye contact as much as I could. I had to make them see. I was confident that I could.
They exchanged another look, I was getting fed up with the underlying atmosphere that something was being left unsaid.
"What is it?" I pushed.
"Well, Tom's refusing the corroborate your story. He says that you might have a history of some mental problems, would you say that was true?"
"No," I said, "That is not true."
"Okay," he replied, "Jim is going to take you into the waiting room. Could you wait there for me? We'll come get you again shortly."

I let Jim lead the way. He didn't say anything at all, just glared at me with a sense of wonder. I was bewildered by the entire situation, like I had just been put into a washing machine and pulled out before the cycle was over. I was back to waiting, sitting on my heels and biting at my dirty fingernails. I wondered if they had called my Mother.

After another little while, a woman appeared. She had a sweet smile, and her face was smooth like silk. Her auburn hair was clipped behind her head. She was dressed older than she looked, in a chiffon shirt and tan cardigan. She introduced herself as Megan.
"Hi Polly, PC Fielding has been telling me about your predicament. I was wondering if we could sit down and talk further about this?"
My mistake was trusting her. I told her everything. She listened intently and kept interjecting with, "that must have been awful for you" and "And what happened next?". I thought we were getting somewhere, and that she was allowing me to offload to someone who might understand.

I was carted off to Fullingham the next morning. They let me stay the night in the cell whilst Megan called my mother, apparently they said that I was in no fit state to make decisions for myself. Fulligham was the best place for me. It was close by, secure, and would give me all the help I needed. My Mum, worried for my welfare, agreed to whatever means necessary. I threw a fit when they tried to put me in the transport, which didn't help my case. I demanded to see my mother, rather than hear second hand what was going on. When you're faced with the unknown, all you want is your mother. They were denying me this request, and I didn't get to see her until I'd been at Fulligham a week so I could "settle in".

We were allowed to meet alone, in a meeting room that smelt sterile. Two leather armchairs sat facing each other, giving you the loose impression that you were sitting in somewhere familiar like your own living room. It certainly didn't feel like that to me.

I explained it all to my Mum. She listened with concern, her chin resting in her palm in a thinking pose. I was visibly traumatised by the experience, if I hadn't been jacked up on drugs I would have been shaking like a wet dog. If I thought about it too deeply, my mind wandered down a dark, narrow alley that made me realise the magnitude of what had happened. My whole life completely upended in a couple of weeks. I would never

go back to the firm. At this rate I would probably never be a lawyer. Tom had ruined my life. I was so numb, that I couldn't even muster the ability to feel vengeful. I was sitting in this chair opposite my Mum, slouched against the back like I'd run out of steam.
"You look tired." Was all she could say.
I stared at her, expressionless.
"Sorry, darling," She sighed, "It's a lot, isn't it? I'm so sorry that happened to you."
"You believe me?" I asked.
"Of course, darling," she leant forward, took my hand, "But we need to give you some time to recover, don't we?"
My Mother had a tell. The corner of her top lip twitched whenever she told a lie. It was fantastic to know when I was a child, but in this moment, it was more of a curse than a blessing. The way she was looking at me, like I was a sick puppy, made me feel vulnerable. She asked me if I resented her for putting me in here, I said I didn't. She told me that they didn't really give her a choice, as I was effectively sectioned. I said that it was fine. There was nothing else I felt I *could* say.
She left me with a kiss on the cheek and a promise she'd be back every Thursday at 10am. Some weeks, if I don't

follow the plan set by Dr Ralph, they tell her she needs to miss a week. She's only ever missed one week. At the beginning she would tell me how lonely she was, but more recently she met a scholar called Graham when she was researching for her new book, and she spends her time with him now sipping coffee and talking about great novelists.

The worst time was when my story got out. Despite my protests, the police refused to do anything further. Tom had vanished into the depths of Cornwall and Clement Ward was not returning emails or calls. He had made his statement, and they believed it. But it seems that one of the orderlies here had loose lips. Within days, I was featured in a weird clickbait article on Facebook. *"Girl, 26, claims she was almost sacrificed by Pagan Cornish Cult."* It gained traction pretty quickly and it was suddenly everywhere. People I knew were sharing calling me crazy, shaming me for being a compulsive liar who'd completely lost the plot. Other papers and blogs started to pick it up, calling it farcical but interesting. There was even a quote from Tom in one of them, who said that I'd become aggressive after he tried to end our engagement and that being in a Psyche

Hospital was the best place for me. Ironically, it was him and his cohort that deserved to be sectioned.

The letters came after that. Flooding in asking me questions about my ordeal. People started making videos about me, investigating the facts and trying to find out the truth. A selfie of me and Tom in 2019 was edited into the thumbnails on videos, looking smiley next to a picture of a bloody knife. People seemed to forget that I was still alive, still feeling the frost in my veins as I was told of another video that had gone viral. It reawakened something every time I looked.

11

There you have it, Jessica. I'm sure this is a lot for you to take in, and I don't want sympathy. I just want someone to look at it from my perspective, and truly believe the words as I say them. You said that you won't edit, and I sincerely hope that you don't. This is in its rawest form.

Until now, I couldn't imagine ever letting my story be published anywhere. I hid away from the media circus, letting people say what they wanted but never getting involved myself. To comment would be to wage a war, knowing that I probably wasn't going to win. I would be inviting the hate, the judgement. I was hiding away in this very room. The truth is, I'm very tired.

So, I will carry on. I'll admit, now this letter is done I am sad that I won't have anything to focus on for a couple of hours each evening. Maybe I will take up writing as a hobby, my Mum would be pleased with that. Maybe when I get out, she can help publish it. Perhaps you could ask the Exeter Herald to endorse it, put me in touch with someone. I'm getting ahead of myself.
I'll go to my group therapy sessions, and I'll eat my muesli. I'll meet with Dr Ralph and tell him all this again, for the 1825th time. He'll tell me I need to let go, I'll refuse, and he'll write up another prescription. Part of me wishes that you could visit, so that you could experience a day with me. I feel weirdly close to you now that I've bore my soul.

They'll turn the lights off in a moment. I can see Mike opening the flap in quicker succession, he's flittering in front of the door as he often does when he's impatient. He wants to go home, relax with his family. The night orderlies will take over, swanning around like ghosts with mugs in their hands and sleep in their eyes. I've said everything I can say.

Before I go, I take one last glance out of the window as the sky fades to black. He stands there, staring back at me from the trees in the distance. His outline, his moonlit face. Leucum Pengally. He looks no different. He follows me, like a curse. I blink, and he's gone again.

Jessica, thank you. Please send me a copy of the finished article when it is completed. Polly Newton, in Room 102.

Best Regards and Signed,

Polly

ACKNOWLEDGEMENTS

I would like to thank my lovely Dad, Alan, and my brother, Robert, for their endless love and support. I just want to make you both proud. Forever grateful to you both.

Thank you to Tony, Shelley & Steve for picking me up and pushing me to publish when I needed it the most.

I would like to thank Carolyn for stepping into my Mum's shoes, and looking after and encouraging me the way she would want you too.

To Alex. Thank you for listening to me endlessly talk about this book. Thank you for being one of the first to read it despite the fact it takes you 1000 years to read a chapter. Thank you for all the love and hope you have given me these past 8 years, and for believing in me when I didn't believe in myself. Always.

Sam, Steph, & Emily. Thank you for being the most fantastic best friends a girl could ask for.

To Louie and Ellie for being the first to read my manuscript after asking for months and months. I cherish you.

My gorgeous friends. We are family. I couldn't have got here without you all.

And finally, to my wonderful Mother, Caroline, with whom this book is dedicated to. You are still my driving force, even if you aren't around to see the rewards. You believed that I could do great things. I hope that, wherever you are, you are proud of your daughter. I love you and I miss you. Always. This was for you.

ABOUT THE AUTHOR

Amy Wonnacott is a 27 year old writer residing on the Sussex coast in Brighton, UK. Amy loves to write fiction and poetry, with her first poem published in a collection at the young age of 7. Writing is her true passion and she loves to take inspiration from the world around her. In her spare time, she loves to lay on the sofa with an episode of Rupaul's Drag Race and cuddle with her little ginger cat, Merlin. With more ideas brewing, watch this space for more stories from this upcoming author.

Printed in Great Britain
by Amazon